"More best man with benefits than friends with benefits?" Nell tilted her head as if she was actually considering it.

"If you like."

"I suppose it could work," she said thoughtfully. "Although there'd have to be some rules."

"I never expected anything less." Nell was the queen of rules and boundaries, after all.

Nell bit down on her lip as she looked up at him. "It's only until after the wedding. Okay? I just... I don't want to risk either of us getting too comfortable in an arrangement that can't last."

"That makes sense," he replied, even as a sinking part of his heart realized that the wedding was only a few weeks away. Why had they wasted the last couple of months dating other people? "We can get it all out of our system between now and then."

"Exactly," Nell said firmly. "Then we can both get back to trying to find real dates we might have a future with."

"Great," Alex said.

Even though, right then, the idea of Nell with another boring date who didn't understand her turned his stomach.

Maybe he could just blame the tequila.

Dear Reader,

This book came about because I told my editor, Megan, that I wanted to write about a couple who were so desperate *not* to have to date each other that they went on a series of worsening dates with awful people...then told each other about them over coffee on Monday mornings.

We had a lot of fun brainstorming the terrible dates and figuring out the logistics of the whole thing. It would be light and fun and frothy—the sort of book I couldn't wait to write and have you read.

And, technically, that's exactly the book I wrote. Except, somewhere along the way, *Best Man with Benefits* became about more than just ridiculous date disasters. It became about the people we choose to be—and how we can't let anyone else make that choice for us. About how love takes courage but that the risk is always worthwhile.

I hope you enjoy Nell's and Alex's adventures in dating. But most of all, I hope that you'll choose, every day, the person that you want to be—and live that life with your whole heart.

Love and confetti,

Sophie x

Best Man with Benefits

Sophie Pembroke

ISBN-13: 978-1-335-59630-7

Best Man with Benefits

Harlequin Enterprises ULC
22 Adelaide St. West, 41st Floor
Toronto, Ontario M5H 4E3, Canada
www.Harlequin.com

Printed in U.S.A.

Sophie Pembroke has been dreaming, reading and writing romance ever since she read her first Harlequin novel as part of her English literature degree at Lancaster University, so getting to write romantic fiction for a living really is a dream come true! Born in Abu Dhabi, Sophie grew up in Wales and now lives in a little Hertfordshire market town with her scientist husband, her incredibly imaginative and creative daughter, and her adventurous, adorable little boy. In Sophie's world, happy *is* forever after, everything stops for tea and there's always time for one more page...

Books by Sophie Pembroke

Harlequin Romance

Dream Destinations

Their Icelandic Marriage Reunion
Baby Surprise in Costa Rica

The Heirs of Wishcliffe

Vegas Wedding to Forever
Their Second Chance Miracle
Baby on the Rebel Heir's Doorstep

Cinderellas in the Spotlight

Awakening His Shy Cinderella
A Midnight Kiss to Seal the Deal

The Princess and the Rebel Billionaire

Visit the Author Profile page
at Harlequin.com for more titles.

To anyone who has ever been set up on a blind date...

Praise for Sophie Pembroke

"An emotionally satisfying contemporary romance full of hope and heart, *Second Chance for the Single Mom* is the latest spellbinding tale from Sophie Pembroke's very gifted pen. A poignant and feel-good tale that touches the heart and lifts the spirits."

—*Goodreads*

CHAPTER ONE

THE OFFICES OF Here & Now Events sat in the centre of London, just off Berkeley Square in Mayfair, in an elegant Georgian townhouse that had been converted into three floors of meeting rooms, desks and display and storage space.

It was also an absolute hotbed of gossip.

As Nell Andrews climbed the few steps to the front door one Monday morning, juggling a heavy laptop bag on one shoulder and the cup of coffee she held in her other hand, she just hoped that her most recent gossip hadn't reached the staff yet.

An assistant, hurrying out of the building despite the early hour, held the door open for Nell and she stepped inside into the familiar soft white space, punctuated with occasional pops of bright celebratory colour. Her own office, up in the attic of the building, stuck to just the white walls and some restful neutrals. But they *were* a party and events company, so a little bit of exciting colour mixed in with the sensible, capable and competent office set-up only made sense. At least that was what Nell's twin sister and business partner, Polly, told her.

Nobody paid Nell much attention as she made her way past the reception space on the ground floor and towards the stairs, passing the display cabinets holding endless party supply samples, and the imposing floral displays that flanked them, in front of the meeting rooms they kept set up for impressing potential clients.

The white walls held oversized canvases showing images from past events, all in black and white except for the odd detail picked out in vivid colour.

Nell turned her head as she passed the largest one, right by the stairs, showing the four of them together at the launch party for Here & Now, five years ago.

Polly, Fred, Alex and Nell.

All rendered in black and white, except for the pink party hat on Polly's head, the green bow tie Fred was wearing, and Alex's purple cummerbund.

Even the photographer hadn't been able to find anything colourful about Nell to edit in.

The four of them had met at university,

where Fred had fallen head over heels for Polly, and she'd kept him dangling at arm's length while she enjoyed the freedom of student life. Fred's best friend, Alex, had regularly been engaged as an envoy to try and get a read on Polly's feelings from Nell, which had brought him into their circle too—especially in second year, when Polly decided it was time to stop playing hard to get, and admit to what everyone else already knew.

Polly and Fred had been madly in love ever since.

And when they announced they wanted to start an events business, after graduation, it had been only natural to bring Nell, Polly's accountant twin sister, and Alex, Fred's law graduate best friend, in to round out the team. Here & Now had been born over a bottle of wine and an Indian takeaway in Nell and Polly's tiny London flat, and from there it had only grown.

Now they had the media mentions, the millionaire clients, the constant referrals from happy customers, the central London offices—and the ever-growing staff.

At the top of the stairs, Nell stepped out into the main office floor—every desk filled by one of those staff members. The office had a constant buzz of chatter, excitement even, as they all went about their days. Organising parties for the rich and famous wasn't the kind of work which lent itself to quiet contemplation. Even now, Nell could see someone holding up two different styles of champagne bottle piñatas for a colleague's approval.

Piñatas? Whose party are those for?

Most of their events were rather more classy than that, but maybe a new client had a sense of fun that outweighed their need to impress. That would make a nice change.

The important thing was, the staff all seemed suitably diverted by their jobs and not at all interested in her. Which hopefully meant the news hadn't got around yet—and even when it did, that nobody would care.

It wasn't as if she was a regular topic of office gossip, she reassured herself. Her life—unlike the lives of almost everyone else who worked for Here & Now—just wasn't interesting enough to gossip about. She made sure of it.

Nell had lived enough drama and high emotion in the first eighteen years of her life to last her for the rest of it. All she wanted now was a quiet, boring, content existence.

Something she'd *thought* she had with Paul. Until this weekend.

There was no real way anyone could know about it yet, was there? Except that the rumour mill at Here & Now was unparalleled, and somehow someone always knew something.

All it would take was Paul telling a friend, who told a friend, who told a cousin, who knew someone who worked at Nell's office, and there it was. Everyone would know.

It wouldn't even have to be Paul. One of her neighbours might have overheard. Or the taxi driver who had to have been eavesdropping on Paul's epic breakup speech, on the drive to the restaurant where, until that moment, Nell had been almost certain he was planning to propose.

Or there was always the other, more exciting, more daring, more *fun* woman that Paul had left her for.

She'd probably told loads of people since Paul had dumped Nell for her on Friday night.

While Nell hadn't quite managed to tell anyone yet. She'd spent the weekend holed up in her tiny flat—the one she used to share with Polly, until the business took off and she and Fred bought their gorgeous house together. She'd stress baked, and watched old episodes of calming shows about country life, where the biggest drama involved whether someone cheated to win the farm show.

And yes, she'd cried. Just a bit.

But not for too long.

After all, if Paul was after excitement and drama, he was the wrong guy for her. Better to know it now than later—after she'd said yes to that non-existent proposal, for example.

She'd picked Paul *because* he was boring like her. Because he was content to stay home on a Saturday night, rather than checking out the latest, hottest club. Because they agreed on everything and never argued. The last thing Nell wanted from a partner was someone who always disagreed with her. Someone she'd spend her life yelling at then making up with.

She wasn't built for that kind of drama. Not like Polly.

Not like their mother or their father.

Nell had always taken after their grandparents more. They would have approved of Paul, she thought. Until now, anyway.

She made it past the dangers of all the desks, and had almost reached the final, narrower staircase that led to her cramped attic office space—away from all the people, sharing the roof space with the storage area—when she heard someone call her name.

'Nell! We're in here! We need you!' Not just someone. Polly.

And when her twin needed her…well. Nell went running. Always had, always would.

She turned and spotted Polly waving at her from the open doorway of the small meeting room they preferred to use for their Core of Four meetings—the term they used for the four of them as owners. And yes, there was Fred, sitting in his customary chair next to where Polly had spread her files and her empty coffee cups across the polished wood of the conference table. And there was Alex too, standing by the window looking out over the leafy street below, his dark russet hair glowing in the weak sun, his hands on his hips, as if reminding them all he had far more interesting and exciting places to be. Because he always did. Always had, even back at university.

Alex McLeod came from money. And land. And possibly some obscure Scottish title.

None of them were under any illusion that he'd agreed to come in on the business for any reason other than his own amusement. He didn't need the income the way normal people did—although Nell supposed it gave him a little petty cash for his regular insane adventures.

She preferred to pay her mortgage and add to her pension, but each to their own.

Fred didn't need the money either, but he did it because this company was Polly's dream, so that was different.

And anyway, she didn't like to spend too much time thinking about Alex. She'd done enough of that in university, and she knew that got her nothing except disappointment. Or embarrassment, and having to avoid each other for one very awkward term, until things had settled down again.

Yes, it was a good job she'd got anything to do with Alex out of her system back in second year. Otherwise working with him would be excruciating.

As it was, she could just avoid him as much as possible, and put a mental lock on that one night where things might have been different.

Nell stepped into the meeting room, sat down in her usual seat and smiled at Fred across the table. Polly, practically vibrating with something—coffee or excitement, Nell wasn't sure—leaned against the back of Fred's chair, hands on his shoulders, as Alex finally deigned to turn around and give them his attention.

'We've got some big news,' Polly said, grinning. 'We're getting married! And we want

Here & Now to arrange the biggest, most amazing wedding ever!'

Alex stared blankly at his best friends and tried to make sense of what they were saying.

'Married. Like...*married* married?' Okay, that didn't even make sense in his own head, and from the derisory look Nell was giving him, he'd just given her another reason to think he was a total waste of space.

He wasn't entirely clear on what her initial reasons for that conclusion were, but he was one hundred per cent sure that she'd made it—probably within the first hour of meeting him at university.

As he recalled, he'd been pretty drunk. That might explain some of it.

And if there had been a time where he thought he might have convinced her otherwise—a time when she might even have *liked* him a little bit...well, that was long past too. He'd ruined that one nice and neatly back in their second year.

But today wasn't a time for dwelling on Nell. Today was about her sister and his best friend.

'Congratulations,' he added, belatedly stepping forward to hug Polly, and clap Fred on the shoulder. 'That's amazing news.'

'It really, really is.' Nell was on her feet too, pulling her twin into a tighter, closer hug than the one he'd given her. 'You'll be settled and together for ever.'

It was easy to forget that Nell and Polly were twins sometimes—they were so different as people. But seeing them with their heads pressed together, matching grins on their faces, Alex was struck afresh by how alike they really looked. Same long dark hair. Same bright blue eyes. Same slender shape and same long fingers clasped together now.

Nell had a dimple in her left cheek that Polly lacked—a dimple Alex had seen but rarely, given how little she smiled in his presence—but otherwise they were identical.

Well, apart from the clothes. There was never any confusion in the office about which twin a staff member was talking to. If she was wearing black, perhaps the odd shade of beige, it was Nell. If there was colour—from a brightly hued silk scarf around her neck to neon-pink high heels, and everything in between—it was definitely Polly.

But now he looked closer, the colours and the dimples weren't the only difference. There was something in the eyes. Polly's held unbridled joy, whereas Nell's…

She was sad. Sad that her sister was getting married? That didn't make any sense.

'So I'm thinking we can really showcase everything we can do through the wedding.' Polly disentangled herself from her sister's arms, settled into her seat and flipped open the first of the folders she'd spread across the table.

Alex laughed. 'We don't even get the engagement story first? Just straight to business?'

Polly rolled her eyes. 'Don't pretend you want all the gory details, Alex. We all know you're fundamentally against the very institution of marriage, but I'm afraid you're going to have to pretend you think it's a good idea for at least a few months, if you're going to be Fred's best man.'

'Which I haven't actually asked him yet, darling,' Fred pointed out sanguinely. It took a lot to ruffle Fred. More than one person in the past—from teachers to women to business acquaintances—had taken that to mean that he didn't care about anything. But Alex knew better than that.

When Fred set his mind on something there wasn't anything in the world that would stop him. He'd fallen in love with Polly the first time he saw her at university, and that had been it for him. He'd never hassled or harassed her, or tried to make her feel guilty for going out with other men. He'd just patiently waited until she came to see the world from his point of view, and realised they were meant to be together.

And now they were getting married.

'Who else would you ask to be best man?' Alex dropped into the fourth chair at the table. 'Nobody else has put up with you for the last twenty-odd years, have they?' Since the day they'd met at boarding school, seven years old and terrified but refusing to show it. 'Anyway, I'm not against marriage *in principle*.'

'Just not for you, right?' Nell's tone was acerbic. Whenever they were all in the same place, Alex couldn't help but feel that Nell thought she saw every inch of his soul and found it sorely lacking.

'Do you really think I'd be an asset to the marriage market?' Alex asked, eyebrows raised, and tried not to be insulted when Polly snorted with laughter.

It *wasn't* that he was against marriage. He truly believed, for instance, that Fred and Polly would have a wonderful marriage. They complemented each other so well, for a start.

People thought Polly was flighty, but she

was just creative. Fred helped her focus her ideas.

And yes, they'd had that whole on-again, off-again thing going on at university, and he'd been party to some ear-splitting arguments between them over the years. But they always made up. Always talked it through and came back together, stronger than before.

He'd had to listen to enough of the aftermath, through shared walls, to know that the arguments weren't *all* bad either. They both definitely enjoyed the making up, anyway.

But for him? He'd thought he'd found love once, but...well. He'd been wrong.

These days, he found fun, excitement and adventure a lot more fulfilling than a bittersweet search for an emotion that might never happen for him. Not everyone found their happy-ever-after. And despite what people—Nell in particular—thought, he wasn't so full of himself to assume he'd be one of the lucky ones, riding off into the sunset with his One True Love.

But that didn't mean he wasn't thrilled to be giving two of his best friends that send-off.

Best man. He'd never been one before. He assumed it came with a bucketload of responsibilities, though—those sorts of titles always did. And the one thing he *did* know about the job of being best man was that he got to flirt with the bridesmaids, right?

Bridesmaids. Wait.

'I assume the lovely Nell will be acting as Maid of Honour opposite me?' he said, the pieces starting to fall into place. Oh, she was going to hate that.

'Of course,' Polly replied. 'Who else would I choose?'

'Right,' Nell said faintly. Alex assumed she was realising the same thing he was. That it was going to be a long, and very busy, few months before the wedding—and they were going to have to spend a lot of time together.

More time than they'd ever spent together since that second year at university, and a night that had changed their friendship for ever.

No wonder Nell looked so horrified.

CHAPTER TWO

NELL'S HEAD WHIRLED with all the ways her world had shifted over the last few days.

Not only was she *not* getting married, Polly was. And Nell was over the moon for her—really, really, she was. Marriage would be good for Polly and Fred, she was sure of it. They loved each other deeply, and perhaps the commitment would help them move past the cycle of arguing and making up they seemed to have fallen into.

Polly always laughed when Nell worried about it. She said that real love needed passion, and she didn't want someone who just said yes to her all the time. Besides, making up was the best part.

But that didn't stop the clenching fear Nell felt in her stomach every time Polly appeared on her doorstep announcing that she couldn't bear to be in the same room as Fred for another moment, so they were having a girls' night.

Their own parents had never managed to get married at all—had barely even lived together. But their mother had married—or almost married—enough times since for Nell to know that a ring and a piece of paper never solved anything.

It would be different for Polly and Fred, though. Because, under it all, they loved each other more than they wanted the drama of the fights and the making up. She was sure of it.

She hoped.

And she was going to be Polly's maid of honour. What did that even entail?

Nell felt a small surge of panic at the idea that she might have to organise a hen do.

Not to mention spending more time with the best man.

Look how that ended up last time we tried it.

It had been years, and she still remembered the heat of her embarrassment and the tightness in her chest in that moment. How close they'd been…and how fast Alex had pulled away from her as the door opened.

Don't think about it. He probably doesn't even remember that night.

Her twin sister didn't seem to notice her reticence. Polly bounced a little in her chair as she turned to Nell. 'I want the whole thing to be a total festival of romance! Like, everything for couples. I'm thinking a fairground with a tunnel of love for the engagement party!'

'Engagement party?' Nell said faintly. 'And you'll want me to—'

'Oh, no!' Polly laughed, tinkling and high and only faintly insulting. 'Don't worry, I'm not expecting you and Alex to do any of the organising or anything. Not when I've got a whole team out there who can do this sort of thing standing on their heads!'

'We'll put the whole thing—engagement party, hen and stag dos, and the wedding week itself—through as a project for the company, just like we were normal clients,' Fred explained.

'That's why I want the couple theme,' Polly added. 'It'll be such a great advert for all the wonderful kinds of events we can provide.'

The couple theme. Right. Nell had been trying to avoid that part.

'About the couple theme...'

'I was thinking maybe all our guests could dress up as famous couples from history or film or whatever for the joint hen and stag do,' Polly burst out. 'Won't that be the most fun?'

'I'm sure it will,' Nell said calmly. 'But, uh,

what about people who don't have another half to invite?'

'Worrying about me, Nell?' Alex tilted his chair back on two legs as he gave her a lazy smile, and Nell scowled back at him. 'I'm sure I can find *someone* to be my plus one.'

'I'm sure you can too, but—' Nell started, only for Polly to cut her off.

'Not just anybody, though,' she told Alex sternly. 'If they're going to be in my wedding photos for all time as the best man's date, I want it to be someone who will actually still be in our lives in six months' time. Otherwise you can pair up with our mother for the occasion, assuming she hasn't remarried already by then.'

Alex looked less pleased at that idea. 'I'm not dating your mother.'

Polly rolled her eyes. 'Of course not. I just meant...oh, you know what I meant.'

'Seldom, if ever,' Alex muttered, and Nell decided it was time to reclaim control of this conversation.

'I wasn't actually talking about Alex,' she said. 'I was talking about me.'

Alex, Fred and Polly all turned to stare at her.

'But you'll be going with Paul,' Polly said, eyes wide with incomprehension.

'Not so much.'

It took pathetically little time to explain what had happened that weekend. Polly's eyes welled up as she threw her arms around Nell, and Nell tried to wriggle out of them.

'I'm fine, really,' she insisted, even if she wasn't completely. She didn't want anyone—not even Polly, and especially not Alex—feeling sorry for her. 'Just…not going to have a partner for your couple-fest.'

To her credit, Polly didn't even suggest that *Nell* partner with their mother. Probably because she knew what a disaster that would be. Chalk and cheese, her grandmother had called them. Her grandfather had used rather stronger terms.

Neither of them had spoken to Nell and Polly's mother in almost a decade, by the time they died.

Polly clapped her hands together, eyes suddenly shining with excitement again. 'No, this is perfect!'

Fred winced at his fiancée's choice of words. 'Maybe not perfect, Pol.'

'Well, no, obviously not *perfect,* perfect. But still pretty great!' Polly grabbed Alex's hand across the table, then reached out for Nell's.

No. No, no, no. Nell could see exactly

where this was going, and she didn't like it one bit. She tried to resist her twin's grip, but it was almost unbreakable when Polly really wanted something.

And it looked like she *really* wanted her couples themed wedding.

I always knew Polly would be a Bridezilla. I just figured it would have more to do with the right shade of flowers or matching dresses than messing with my love life.

'You and Alex can just pair up for all the events!' Polly said gleefully, and Nell's heart finished its long, slow drop towards her shoes. 'That way, he can't bring some date whose name he doesn't even know, and you won't be *alone*.'

The stress she put on the last word made it sound like a fate worse than death.

But it wasn't, Nell knew. It was far, far worse to be with the wrong person than alone.

And Alex McLeod was most definitely the wrong person. She'd learned that years ago.

She couldn't find a nicer way to say it. Couldn't mind Alex's feelings. Couldn't even keep the words in.

'Not a chance in hell,' Nell blurted, too loud and too fast, and across the table Alex laughed at her.

Oh, yes. This really was the perfect day.

* * *

'Nell!' Polly sounded genuinely offended on his behalf, which Alex supposed he should be grateful for. But really, it was kind of a ridiculous idea.

'Polly, Nell and I are not going to start dating just to make your wedding pleasingly symmetrical,' he said, as drily as he could manage under the circumstances.

Of course he and Nell weren't going to couple up. If that had ever been going to happen, it would have done so back at university, during that week in second year when they'd…connected. When it had almost felt like there'd been a chance for them. Something between them worth exploring.

But it *hadn't* happened, and that was for the best, given how their lives had turned out, the people they'd grown into. They were polar opposites. Of *course* they weren't going to get together now.

Did Nell really need to sound *quite* so repulsed by the idea, though?

Polly rolled her eyes. 'I'm not suggesting that either of you are likely to fall madly in love with each other in the three months it's going to take to plan this wedding—'

'Three months?' Nell interjected. 'Don't

most weddings take, well, a year or more to plan?'

Her twin gave her a withering look. Alex was glad he wasn't the only person who got that one directed at him. 'We're professionals, Nell. And I have some strings I can pull with suppliers and venues.'

'Still, three months...' Nell shook her head, her long dark hair slipping over her shoulders. Alex suspected she was doing calculations in her head—of how much extra they'd pay for the short notice, or the overtime it was going to take.

Even if this was a Here & Now project, Nell would still be handling the money side. His expertise would only be needed for checking contracts—and maybe writing a prenup, if Fred and Polly had any sense. Which, in his experience, they didn't. Not when it came to love.

'The point is, neither of you are likely to find *anyone* to fall madly in love with in the next three months,' Polly went on. 'But I don't want either of you bringing just anybody to my wedding. Apart from anything else, we're planning on a destination wedding out in the Seychelles. If you fall out with your date there it's a long way home.'

She was looking directly at Alex as she said

it and he knew, without having to ask, that she was remembering the time he'd brought a girl he'd just met to their New Year's Eve celebration at some cottage in the hills they'd hired, and then she'd dumped him just before midnight but they'd had to spend the new year together anyway, because they were in the middle of nowhere and everyone was over the alcohol limit for driving.

Yeah, maybe she had a point. He really didn't want to go through that again.

'And you want people who are still in your life in the photos,' Nell said wearily. 'I get that. But I'm pretty sure there's another way round this.'

Lots, probably, Alex figured. But once Polly had got a path set in her mind it was hard to lead her off it. One of the ways she and Fred were alike, he supposed.

God help them all when they picked different paths. The showdowns were epic.

'Three months is plenty of time to find love,' Alex said definitively, even though he had no real idea if it was true. Nell clearly didn't want to spend any more time with him than she had to, and he wasn't exactly keen either. If he wanted to be a disappointment to people, he'd go home and visit his parents more often.

But they were going to have to work together to get out of this. Fortunately, Nell picked up on his theme instantly. 'Some people get engaged within three months. Or even married.'

'And haven't you ever heard of love at first sight?' Alex added.

'Exactly!' Nell said, then frowned. 'Wait...'

'Nell doesn't believe in love at first sight,' Polly said smugly.

'Three months isn't first sight, though,' Fred said thoughtfully. 'I mean, they're not wrong. I fell in love with you faster than that. It just took you a little longer to realise what I already knew.'

Polly rolled her eyes. 'Fine. Here's the deal. Either the two of you pair up for the wedding events, or you *both* find another partner to bring—but no fake dates, and nobody you've just met. It doesn't have to be your forever person—I'm not expecting miracles. But it has to be someone you genuinely believe you have a chance with. Okay?'

Alex and Nell exchanged a quick glance, then nodded. But something about the look in Polly's eye told Alex he was being set up here, even if he wasn't entirely sure what for. She said she didn't expect miracles, but was this Polly's way of trying to get them both as coupled up and settled down as she and Fred were?

Surely she knew him better than that by now? Alex was not the settling kind.

He knew how miserable that could make a man, after all.

'And if you don't have anyone by the time the hen and stag dos are done and dusted, you're coming together,' Polly finished. 'Now, onto more important things. Like planning my wedding! Let's get the whole team in here and share the news!'

CHAPTER THREE

THE STAFF, it seemed, already knew exactly what was going on—because they exploded into the too-small meeting room with trays of Buck's Fizz and the champagne bottle piñatas Nell had spotted before. She kept herself pressed against the wall as the excitement filled the room to bursting point. She had no idea how news had got around so fast, only that it always did at Here & Now.

Fred fired up a slideshow on the big screen, filled with Polly's wedding mood boards, and it was clear by the way the team started shouting out possible ideas that this was going to go on awhile. The brainstorming section of a new project was always the loudest and most enthusiastic part of the process.

Nell was just wondering if she could escape up the stairs to her quiet attic office when she felt a tug on her arm.

'You know, I'm thinking we're surplus to requirements here right now,' Alex murmured, leaning close enough to her ear that she could feel his breath against her skin. She forced herself to repress a shiver at the sensation. 'What do you say we go have a strategy session of our own, best man to maid of honour?'

'Can it be somewhere with coffee?' Nell asked. The cup she'd bought on her way in was long gone, and she could already tell this day was going to require a lot of caffeine.

'Most definitely.'

Neither Polly or Fred seemed to notice as they slipped out of the meeting room and hurried down the stairs. Nell felt a pang of guilt about leaving the wedding planning session, but only a small one. Polly knew exactly what she wanted, and she had assembled the right team to make it happen, exactly to her specifications. Other than handling the financial and legal aspects, she and Alex were surplus to requirements. And right now it was all about the ideas. Polly would call them in when they got down to the details.

Outside, the spring morning was warm—one of the first truly warm days of the year. Nell was glad she'd left her coat in the meeting room; she wouldn't need it. Or her laptop or files, she supposed—all of which were tucked under the table back at the office. All she had with her was her phone, and it felt strange to be so unencumbered on a work day. Like she was playing hooky from school—not that she'd ever actually done that. But she imagined the feeling was much the same. She hoped she didn't have any video meetings this morning that she'd forgotten about…

She pulled her calendar up on her phone to check, and Alex rolled his eyes.

'Put that thing away and live dangerously with me for a moment, would you?'

'I thought that was exactly what we were strategising to avoid,' Nell replied archly.

'Good point,' Alex said. 'Check away.'

They strolled along the leafy Mayfair street until they reached Hyde Park, pausing at the first coffee stand they came to. Alex bought their drinks, and Nell sipped at hers as they walked.

'Straight black Americano,' she said, surprised. He hadn't asked for her order. 'How did you know?'

'I do notice some things,' he replied. 'And besides. You're a straight black coffee kind of woman.'

'Boring, you mean.' It wasn't as if she didn't know how he felt about her. Had known for plenty of years now.

'No-nonsense,' he countered. 'Now. What

the hell is going on with Polly and this couples retreat of a wedding idea?'

Nell sighed. 'I have no idea.' Except that wasn't *entirely* true. She'd been Polly's closest companion and confidante their whole lives—well, until Fred, anyway. She knew how her sister's mind worked. 'I suspect it's that she's happy, and she wants everyone else she loves to have the same happiness.'

'And so she's trying to get us both to couple up. With each other.' Alex sounded sceptical, which was fair enough. They weren't exactly an obvious pairing.

Even if Polly didn't know that they'd already tried and failed before.

'Or with anyone.' She shrugged. 'It's more of an emotional instinct with her, rather than a conscious decision.' That was the way Polly always did everything—on instinct, just like their mother. While Nell, on the other hand, would spend weeks working out the pros and cons, weighing up her options, before making the safest choice.

'Well, I suppose it's nice that she wants us to be happy.' The doubt in his voice suggested otherwise, but Nell didn't call him on it.

'So all we really need to do is show her that we *are* happy, and she'll leave us alone.' Put like that, it didn't seem so impossible.

'And have dates for her couples-only wedding events,' Alex pointed out. Okay, that part was a little harder.

They walked through the park in silence for a minute, each lost in their own thoughts as they drank their coffee.

'*Are* you happy?' Alex asked suddenly.

Nell, halfway through a sip, spluttered coffee down her top. Thank goodness her signature black sweater didn't show it.

For a moment he'd sounded the way he had during that week in second year, just after Fred and Polly had finally got together and the two of them were left out in the cold. They'd talked—really talked—about things other than her sister and his best friend for the first time. And she'd believed, for a short while, that maybe he was really interested in what she had to say.

One week where they'd connected as human beings. And one night where the whole idea of them as friends—or more—had been smashed to pieces.

It was too late to resurrect that fledgeling friendship now, surely?

'Sorry.' Alex fished a handkerchief—a real, old-fashioned cotton one—from his pocket and handed it to her. 'I just meant...you got dumped this weekend. It would be perfectly normal not to be happy.'

'I did not get dumped,' Nell lied. 'We just realised we wanted different things out of life, so agreed to go our separate ways.' Paul wanted excitement and drama, and she wanted anything but. Easy decision, really.

The fact he'd already fallen in love with another woman was really beside the point when you looked at it that way.

From the pitying look Alex was giving her, she suspected he was seeing it the more traditional way.

'Fine,' she said. 'I got dumped. But it was honestly all for the best. And it definitely doesn't mean I need you to take me to the wedding as a pity date, okay?'

'I kind of got that from your reaction to the suggestion. What was it again? Oh, yes.' He put on a voice that didn't sound a bit like her. '*"Not a chance in hell."* Pretty clear.'

'Oh, like you'd want to go with me anyway,' Nell replied. 'I'd be your worst nightmare as a date.'

Pausing on the path, Alex looked her up and down, then shrugged. 'I don't see why. You're intelligent, funny when you don't think people are listening, and you're objectively gorgeous. I could do worse.'

Nell ignored the way her heart thumped twice at 'objectively gorgeous'. Yes, she looked exactly like Polly, so she knew she didn't look bad or anything. But where Polly wore her looks with charm and grace and smiles, Nell… didn't. *Objectively* was the key word here.

On paper, she was a catch. In practice…

She already knew how he reacted to the idea of kissing her in practice.

That night lived in infamy in her memory. If she concentrated, she was right back there in his university bedroom, sitting beside Alex on the bed after a week of getting to know each other as more than extensions of Fred and Polly. Maybe they hadn't shared all their deepest secrets, but they'd connected in a way she'd never expected to.

And then they'd connected in another way. Tipsy and relaxed, they'd kissed and kissed, and she'd started to think for the first time that this could be more… Until the door had opened and Fred and a few of his other mates had yelled something about needing his help, calling for him to join them—and Alex had pulled away fast, darting to the door before they saw him with her. Because Alex McLeod didn't kiss boring, sensible girls like Nell Andrews.

Then he was gone, the door slamming behind him. She'd waited briefly, then headed back to her own room, telling herself it was all for the best. Alex McLeod was not a good fit for the life she wanted to lead, anyway. And they'd never mentioned the kiss again.

'Doesn't matter,' she said, knowing exactly how to shut this conversation down. 'You'd never date me, because I'm too boring for you.' End of story.

Except, to her surprise, this time it wasn't.

Boring?

Alex steered them towards the nearest bench and sat down beside her, surveying her in light of her words. From the shiny sleek black hair that flowed over her shoulders, to the intelligence in the light blue eyes behind her tortoiseshell glasses, down over her signature black sweater and trousers, to her polished black heeled boots. Nell, for her part, sipped at her coffee and awaited his judgement.

But this wasn't about her looks, or the person she presented to the world, was it?

It was about who she believed she was, inside.

'You *want* to be boring,' he realised suddenly. 'You are actively trying to be boring.'

Her gaze slid away from his and she shrugged,

and the boring black sweater slipped from her shoulder—just an inch or two, before she yanked it back up—but long enough to give him a flash of a bright pink bra strap.

And a memory. Of walking into Polly's and Nell's university rooms looking for Fred, and finding Nell in a tired old bathrobe that wasn't tied quite tightly enough to hide the teal and pink leopard print lingerie she was wearing under it.

He'd thought it was Polly, until she'd walked in arm in arm with Fred. Because surely *Polly* was the twin who'd wear the daring lingerie, while Nell would wear sensible cotton basics.

But apparently not. And apparently there was still some of that girl inside her, even now.

The girl who'd once kissed him like the world was ending. Like he could fall into her and never come out.

Who'd then run away and ignored him afterwards, and pretended it had never happened.

No, Nell wasn't boring. She was a veritable puzzle box he wasn't sure he'd ever understand.

Maybe this wedding was the universe giving him a chance to do just that.

'I'm not trying to be anything,' Nell said,

but he could hear the lie in her voice. 'This is just who I am.'

'Maybe who you are isn't as boring as you think.'

Oh, not because of whatever she wore underneath her perma-black outfits—or because of any years-ago memory of one drunken night at university. But because he saw that spark in her eye whenever a staff member said something ridiculous, and he knew she wanted to mock it but didn't. He'd seen her, for years now, standing on the sidelines of life, never quite giving herself to it—but he could tell there was a part of her that wanted to.

He'd spent enough time with her ex, Paul, at events over the past couple of years to have been baffled as to what she saw in him. There was no connection between them, the way there was between Fred and Polly—an intuitive link that even an outsider could see. No obvious chemistry either, from the dry hello or goodbye kisses he'd witnessed. And nothing in Paul's less than sparkling conversation or company to explain it either.

He was good enough looking, Alex supposed, but that had never seemed to be what mattered most to Nell anyway.

Even Polly had been at a loss to explain

the relationship, but they'd been together for two full years, so there must have been something. She must have loved him, he supposed.

Now he was out of the picture, would she be willing to let that not at all boring side out?

Alex wasn't sure.

So he went back to the only thing he *was* certain about.

'So, this wedding. If we don't want to go together, we're going to have to find other dates.'

Nell nodded. 'I was thinking about this. They really don't have to be our forever person or whatever, do they?'

'I don't think I even *want* a forever person, let alone to have to try and find one in three months just to look good in some photos.' Alex had always heard that planning a wedding did something to a person's logic faculties, but Polly already seemed to be taking it to a new level.

If he didn't know how madly in love Polly and Fred really were, he'd be thinking this was all a publicity stunt for the company. Not that they needed it.

'All we really need to do is find plausible dates. People they believe we could really fall for,' Nell went on. 'I mean, if she's worried about the photos we could just appear together in those, right?'

'Sure,' Alex said with a shrug. 'If you're sure you can put up with standing next to me long enough for a camera shutter to close a few times.'

Nell elbowed him lightly in the stomach. 'You're taking this way too personally.'

'You not wanting to date me? Why would that be personal?'

'You don't want to date me either,' she pointed out, which was hard to argue with.

'I don't like being told who to date,' he said. 'And it's not like I couldn't find my own date for a wedding.'

'So we'll do just that.' Nell gave him a mischievous smile that made him think of leopard print lingerie again. 'Operation Wedding Date.'

'We're *naming* it now?'

'Whatever it takes to get it done.'

Alex sighed. 'Fine. So we both find another date to take to this wedding as fast as possible—'

'One that fits with Polly's rules,' Nell broke in. 'She'll know if it's a fake date or whatever. I don't know how, but she will. She *always* knows.'

He knew Polly well enough not to argue

that one. Her intuition was scary sometimes. 'A *real* date, then. Someone she will believe could be the real thing for us.'

Maybe he even would be, for Nell. There had to be someone out there better for her than Paul, anyway. Perhaps this wedding would give her the push she needed to find him.

Because Alex was almost sure that Nell was anything but boring, and she needed a partner who brought that out in her.

It just wasn't going to be Alex. That ship had sailed years ago. And maybe she wasn't boring, but Nell didn't want the kind of life he led. And he didn't want any life that meant succumbing to the sort of misery his parents had made of marriage.

'Exactly.' Nell nodded, and stuck out her hand. 'Let's do this, then.'

Placing his coffee cup down on the bench, he took her hand and shook it.

Operation Wedding Date was a go.

CHAPTER FOUR

AGREEING TO OPERATION WEDDING DATE in principle was all very well, but when it came to actually putting it into practice Nell found it easier to, well, not.

It wasn't like her sister was going to un-invite her to the wedding if she didn't have a satisfactory date, she reasoned. Plus, if she found one too soon she'd have to date him for the whole three months until the wedding, and she wasn't sure she was ready for that, so soon after Paul's betrayal.

Trusting a man enough to take him to a wedding was one thing. Trusting him enough to actually date him for real, and imagine a future together…that was going to take a little longer.

So she pushed it to the back of her mind for the next week, and concentrated on the business side of making the wedding happen at all—not to mention the finances for all their other projects at Here & Now.

As a strategy, procrastination was serving her well until she found herself round at Polly and Fred's lovely townhouse for dinner the following weekend. She was happily sitting on the sofa with a glass of wine, leafing through one of Polly's many bridal magazines, when her sister launched her attack.

'So, how is the date-finding mission going?' Polly asked, plonking herself down on the sofa beside Nell, her laptop tucked under her arm.

Nell narrowed her eyes. The laptop was suspicious.

'I've got plenty of time,' she said. 'I don't want to just rush into something. You were very clear that you only want me to bring someone I think I could have a future with, after all.'

Using Polly's own arguments against her was the only way to ever win in a disagreement with her twin, in Nell's extensive experience.

'You're right.' Polly flipped open her computer on her lap, and angled the screen towards Nell. 'You need someone who is totally compatible with you from the start. Which is why I've signed you up to this new dating website one of our clients has developed. It has the greatest accuracy on personal traits and beliefs ever! Fred and I road tested it for them, and it matched us up instantly.'

'Which is more than Polly managed,' Fred threw in from the kitchen, where he was cooking them all dinner.

'You...signed me up?' Nell stared at the screen, and the happy smiling couple on it. They didn't look anything like the way she felt in a relationship. Apart from anything else, they were apparently about to dive off a cliff together.

Without helmets. Or a safety rope. Or any information about the depth of the water below, or possible rocks awaiting them.

'I'm not sure this is my kind of dating site.' She pushed the computer back towards Polly.

Polly pushed it back again. 'Of course it is. It's for everybody! It says right here at the top, see?'

What it actually said was, *There's somebody out there for everybody!* The *Even you, you loser,* was unwritten but still clear.

Nell sighed. 'You already signed me up. Did you do all the questionnaires and things as well?'

'Of course.' Polly grinned. 'You always say I know you better than yourself.'

This was true. But it didn't stop Nell feeling… What *was* she feeling? As if her whole personality and life had been decided for her by some test on a dating site. As if her existence was…static. Unchanging and unchangeable.

Which was fine, really. Nell had decided who she wanted to be a long time ago, and could summarise it easily enough. *Not my mother.*

Not the woman who flitted around the world from one adventure, one lover—one *drama*—to another, leaving her daughters behind with grandparents who resented them. Not the woman who always, always had to be the centre of attention. Who used her beauty and her charm and her vibrancy to make the world love her, even as she used it to her own ends.

Polly had got the best parts of Madeline Andrews. Not just her beauty and her charm, but her openness. Combined with an authenticity and empathy that their mother had never shown, Polly just drew people in and made them love her. If she liked being the centre of attention sometimes, or lived her life with flair and drama, that was okay—because she'd be just as likely to make someone else the centre of things, and use her powers of persuasion and partying for others too.

Maybe that was why nobody was objecting to the over-the-top wedding celebrations they had planned.

But Nell…she'd inherited her mother's looks too, but not the charm to go with them. She had the calculating brain, the way to look at any situation and figure out how to use it to her advantage. She just didn't want to use it that way, so she kept it for spreadsheets and figures.

She didn't want to be the centre of anything. She didn't want a life filled with drama.

She wanted the safety and security that Madeline had never, ever been able to offer them.

'You are actively trying to be boring,' Alex had said. And maybe he was right.

But what was so wrong with that?

She scrolled down the screen to the answers Polly had given for her. In many ways, they were spot-on—her twin really did know her better than she knew herself. But every few questions she came across an answer that jarred.

'My ideal date is a cruise along the Seine?' Nell raised her eyebrows at her sister.

Polly shrugged. 'Paris is romantic.'

'And I'd love to go for dinner at a rooftop restaurant? You do remember I'm afraid of heights?'

'You're afraid of everything,' Polly said, not unkindly. 'But in love sometimes you have to take a chance. Jump off that cliff, so to speak.'

'What if I don't want to?'

'Then you'll have to come to my wedding with Alex,' Polly said.

'Right.' The only thing worse than going on a series of set up dates through a dating site had to be attending the wedding of the year as Alex McLeod's pity date, knowing that everyone else there knew he was only taking her because no one else would.

That was not happening.

Polly obviously read her decision on her face because she said, 'Okay, then. Let's look through these matches. I want you booked on a date every weekend between now and the hen night before Fred finishes cooking the curry. All right?'

And, despite all her many, many reservations, Nell nodded.

It wasn't that Alex didn't want to find a date for Polly and Fred's wedding, it was just that there was no real rush. Three months wasn't long to find someone he'd actually plan to spend the rest of his life with—three years wasn't long enough for that. Or nearly thirty, going on present evidence.

But to find someone compatible enough that he could date them for the couple of weeks between the stag do and the wedding? No problem. He and Nell would pair up for the photos, Polly would be too busy getting married to really care, and everything would be fine.

Really, there was no rush at all. And that was why he wasn't rushing.

And why he was surprised that Fred brought it up at all the weekend following the engagement announcement.

He and Fred had a standing once a month Sunday meet-up. Some months they caught a rugby match, some they met old friends at the pub, and some they drove out of the city and went rock-climbing. This month was a rock-climbing month.

Fred waited until they'd almost reached the peak of the ledge they were climbing before he mentioned it.

'So, do you have a date for the wedding yet?'

Alex, concentrating on getting his next hand hold, and bringing his leg up behind him safely, ground out a succinct, 'No.'

'Time's getting short.' Fred swung himself up over the ledge to sit at the top. He'd been practising, probably at that indoor wall not far from the office. Alex should do that too, except he didn't want to. He liked climbing outdoors, where the risk and danger felt real, far more than indoors with all the safety measures and security indoor walls required.

'There's three months to go.'

'Less now,' Fred said. 'And, well, Polly's getting anxious.'

Ah, so that explained it. *Polly* was worked up about it, which meant Fred had to be bothered too, or she'd take her ire out on him. If he talked to Alex, though, she could transfer all that annoyance to him and spare her fiancé.

Fantastic. So he was the fall guy.

Not a thought he wanted to be having as he hung from a rock ledge, really quite far up off the ground.

He swung himself up behind Fred, panting a little as he sat beside him.

God, he loved this spot. Far enough away from the city that he felt in another world. As much as he loved London's cut and thrust and busy, busy, busy—and, he had to admit, he really loved its restaurants and other entertainments—there was something about being out in the country. About breathing in clear air, watching the clouds pass over trees and hills rather than skyscrapers. About hearing the sounds of nature rather than cars and cell phones.

'So?' Fred asked again, and Alex revised his view of being out in the middle of nowhere.

If he was in London, having this conversation on his mobile, he could duck into the tube and lose Fred instantly. Instead, here he was, actually having to answer questions about his love life.

'I haven't given the matter much thought just yet,' he replied. 'Not everyone looks at a woman and knows she'll be the love of his life, you realise.'

Fred and Polly's story was one of a kind—almost like a movie romance. And Alex had loved watching it, in a way he never liked the *actual* romcoms Polly sometimes insisted on for movie night.

They complemented each other in ways Alex had never really imagined people could. His own experience of marriage and relationships came mostly from his parents' marriage, and he had only come to realise as an adult that that really wasn't typical.

His parents would argue and storm out and refuse to speak for months, his mother relocating to one of their other houses—often with another, younger lover his father pretended not to know about—before returning in a sea of apologies and gifts, usually when she'd run out of spending money. They'd make up—loudly and often in front of guests—before retiring to the bedroom for a day or two. And then it would all start again…

When Fred and Polly had an argument, they just kept going. They argued until they were each blue in the face—but they'd come to see each other's point of view in the end, even if they never actually agreed with it. Eventually, they'd come to a compromise.

And nobody ever left—at least, not for more than a night, when Polly decided an argument was stupid and she needed a girls' night, and Fred called Alex over to drink beer and not talk about it. Then, in the morning, Polly would be back, and it would be over.

The making up was equally obnoxious, but somehow Alex found he didn't mind so much, when it was them.

Now, sitting on a rock face miles away from his fiancée, Fred sighed. 'Look, you know I don't care about this. You want to be alone for ever, that's fine by me—you can be sad Uncle Alex to my kids one day.'

'Or fun Uncle Alex who doesn't have to worry about the responsibilities of kids or a spouse or anything like that.'

'If you like,' Fred acquiesced easily. 'But for the next three months—just the next three months—you have to pretend like love and romance is the most wonderful thing in the world. For Polly. And for me, because she'll give me hell if you don't.'

Alex sighed. Three months. He could give his friends three months of make-believe, he supposed. 'Don't worry. I'll find a date.'

'You know, Polly set Nell up on this dating site we road-tested for one of our clients,' Fred said. 'She's got dates every weekend between now and the stag and hen party already. I could get you the details, if you wanted.'

Alex wasn't sure what rankled more. The idea that he needed the help of a website to find dates, or that Nell already had a full roster of them. She certainly hadn't wasted any time—which had to be an indication of how much she really didn't want to go to this wedding with him.

For a second, an image of Nell sitting beside him on that bench, sipping her coffee, as her sweater slipped just enough to give him a glimpse of bright pink bra strap, flashed through his mind—along with a question.

What would it take to get her to give up trying to be boring?

More to the point, what might he discover if she did?

Alex shook the thought away, and pulled out his phone. He'd been there, tried that, and it had been a disaster. Nell had barely spoken to him for the rest of that year, after their kiss, she'd been so horrified by their actions.

'I can get a date any time I want,' he said, scrolling through his contacts. 'Trust me.'

He found the one he was looking for, and hit the call button.

'Hey, Annabel?' he said when she answered. 'Alex McLeod here. We met at that gallery opening last month? I know we talked about getting together sooner, but things have been manic.' He paused to let her say that her life had been the same, and they laughed together at the craziness of London life. They both knew this dance. 'Reason I was calling, I have to fly to New York this weekend for an event, and I wondered if you might like to join me? My treat, of course. Great! I'll send you the flight details as soon as I have them, and arrange a car to the airport. Can't wait.'

He hung up and glanced across at Fred, who didn't look quite as impressed as Alex thought he should.

'See? Easy.'

CHAPTER FIVE

NELL SPENT THE next week alternately panicking about, and trying to think of ways to get out of, the first date the agency had set her up with, on Saturday night. But in the end she decided there was nothing for it but to just go with it and hope for the best. After all, the agency knew what they were doing. Right?

Apparently not.

'It can't have been that bad,' Polly said the following Monday morning, when she cornered her in the office kitchen to hear all about the date.

'It was worse,' Nell replied shortly. 'Now, are you going to let me at the coffee or not?'

Polly moved directly in front of the coffee machine. 'Not until you tell me what happened.'

'You remember that rooftop restaurant idea you put in my profile? I can confirm that it was *not* a good idea.'

Her sister winced. 'Your fear of heights

kicked in? I was hoping the romantic atmosphere would distract you.'

'And maybe it would have. If we'd ever got there.' Nell feinted right then darted left, hoping to trick Polly into giving up the caffeine. It didn't work.

Sometimes it really seemed like her twin could read her mind—usually when she didn't want her to. Of course, other times it felt like she didn't understand her at all…

'Are we having the post weekend date chat in here?'

Nell spun around to find Alex lounging against the doorframe behind her. 'Girl talk,' she said shortly. 'Nothing you'd be interested in.'

'Oh, I don't know,' Alex replied. 'After the disaster of a date *I* had this weekend, I'd quite like to hear someone else's tale of woe for a change.'

'You had a bad date too?' It was hard to imagine, really. In her head everything in Alex's life went exactly according to plan. And if it didn't, it was only because a bigger, better, more dramatic adventure had come along.

Alex glanced between her and Polly, obviously taking in the coffee standoff. 'Come on. I'll buy you a coffee and you can tell me all about your weekend.'

Nell considered for a moment. On the one hand, it meant confessing her dating disaster to Alex McLeod. But, on the other, she'd get one over on Polly *and* get coffee.

Put like that, it was a no-brainer.

'Come on, then.'

A short stroll down the road and past the daffodils and crocuses blooming at the edge of the park, and they were back at the same coffee cart they'd stopped at the other day.

'So, what happened?' Alex asked as they waited for their drinks. 'On your date, I mean.'

Nell sighed at the memory. 'When Polly filled in my dating profile, she said that my idea of a really romantic date was dinner in a rooftop restaurant, looking out over the city.'

'Sounds good to me.'

'Then you're obviously not cripplingly afraid of heights.'

He winced. 'Ah. Not ideal.'

They both took their coffees and moved away, almost instinctively, towards the bench they'd occupied last time.

'As it happened, it didn't matter,' Nell went on. 'Because the lift to the top floor broke down halfway up, and we were stuck in it for three hours waiting for the fire brigade to come and break us out.'

Alex spluttered coffee over the path. 'Three

hours? In a lift? Wait, aren't you equally not fond of small places?'

'Well remembered,' she said drily. 'A hangover from a childhood game of hide and seek gone very wrong.'

'I suppose at least it gave you and your date time to get to know one another?' Alex said, clearly hunting desperately for some sort of silver lining.

'Not really. Turns out he was claustrophobic too, so we mostly had private breakdowns in our own corners of the lift.' It had been, hands down, the most disastrous date of her life. Not that she had very many to compare it to. But still, it reaffirmed her belief that staying home alone was much safer than 'putting herself out there' as Polly kept insisting she did.

Alex leaned back against the bench, his long legs stretched out in front of him, his face contemplative. 'What?' she asked. 'You've got a look. What're you thinking?'

'A look? Me?' Alex attempted what she assumed he thought an innocent face looked like, and failed miserably. She raised her eyebrows and he gave up. 'Fine. I was just thinking that if I was stuck in a lift with someone I found attractive for three hours on a first date… I'm pretty sure I could find a way to pass the time.'

He meant having sex, Nell realised, heat crawling up her neck. Because in Alex's world, that was the kind of thing that happened. Random sex with a semi-stranger in a broken-down lift, with the fire brigade about to arrive any moment.

It was so far away from her world that the idea hadn't even crossed her mind. And she was pretty sure it hadn't crossed her date's mind either, given the way he'd been whimpering in the corner.

Maybe they should have tried it. It might have distracted them both from their impending breakdowns.

But no. That was the sort of thing that her mother might do. Or Polly and Fred.

Not Nell.

It was…anti-Nell behaviour. And from the smirk on Alex's face he knew that.

Knew it from personal experience too. Although if he'd hung around instead of running off with his mates that night at university, to avoid the humiliation of people knowing he'd been kissing her, who knew what might have happened?

Nothing good, she thought darkly. Well,

maybe good in the moment, but not for the long term.

And she wasn't a 'good in the moment' sort of person. They both knew that.

'So what went wrong with your date?' she asked, eager to change the subject.

Alex groaned. 'Trust me, it was way worse than getting stuck in a lift for three hours.'

'Really?' It was hard to imagine *any* date being worse than that one.

'Come on.' He jumped to his feet and dumped his empty coffee cup in the nearby bin. 'We can enjoy the spring flowers while you mock me for my date from hell.'

Perhaps, Alex had decided, New York had been a little ambitious for his first outing of Operation Wedding Date. But he wasn't the sort of guy to do things by halves, and women loved a big gesture, didn't they?

Like a rooftop restaurant, he supposed.

They'd been unlucky with the lift, but from Nell's expression as she'd told him about it, it didn't sound as if she had any intention of seeing the guy again. There was no coming back from mutual breakdowns on a first date, really.

Still. The part he couldn't get his head around was that the guy had been trapped with *Nell* for three hours and hadn't even got some flirting in. Granted, the claustrophobia probably hadn't helped, but still. Three hours. He'd have definitely tried for a kiss to take her mind off things, or something.

He knew how she kissed, after all.

It made a much better story too.

Far superior to his New York one, anyway.

'So who was she?' Nell asked as they rounded a bed of some purple flowers or another. He'd never really understood gardening, and the seasons came so much earlier down here than they did at home in Scotland, he wouldn't know what to look for when, anyway. 'Blind date? Old friend? An ex?'

'Someone I met at a gallery opening a few weeks ago,' he replied. 'We exchanged numbers at the time and then, well, life got busy, and neither of us called.'

'Until now.'

'Well, Fred was nagging me about getting a date for the wedding. So I gave her a call and asked if she'd like to come to New York with me for the weekend.'

It took him a couple of steps to realise that Nell had stopped walking. 'New York?' she said incredulously when he turned around to find her.

He shrugged. 'It seemed like a good idea at the time.'

'You really don't do things by halves, do you?' Nell shook her head, but started walking again at least. It wasn't quite warm enough just yet to do a lot of standing around.

'I was going anyway,' he explained. 'There was this party… Anyway, it doesn't matter, because we never made it.'

'To the party?'

'To New York.'

'What happened?' Nell's eyes were wide with anticipation, and something about the expression made Alex want to live up to her expectations. To spin a good story—even if the ending was rather pathetic.

He hooked her arm through his and led her around the longer path that would eventually lead them back to the office—just not too quickly. Normally, he was keen to get his work done and clock off for the day to enjoy his free evenings for flirting, friends, partying, or whatever. But, for some reason, today felt like a day to take a longer coffee break with Nell, and work late that evening to make up for it.

Alex decided not to read too much into that feeling.

'So, picture it. It's a Friday night in London, and the rain is lashing down. I pull up outside a Chelsea townhouse in a limo—'

'Because who wants understated on a first date?' Nell interjected.

'Exactly. So I'm in my limo, wearing my best suit, ready to jet off to the city that never sleeps with a beautiful woman on my arm.'

'Because you wouldn't take her if she wasn't beautiful.' There was something in Nell's voice that gave him pause, but he wasn't quite sure what it was. After all, *she* was beautiful. At least he thought so.

'I only meet beautiful women,' he said instead. 'Or maybe I just think all women are beautiful.' That hadn't occurred to him before. But really, it was hard to think of a woman he'd ever met who hadn't had *something* beautiful about her. Never the same things—he wasn't one of those men who had a type and stuck to it with religious fervour. But there was always something.

Like with Nell, it was the waterfall of dark hair over her shoulders, the knowing, mocking eyes behind her glasses, the curved lines of her that ran from her shoulder, in at her waist and back out over her hips…

Okay, maybe Nell had more beauty about her than most women. But every woman had *something*.

'Fine. Carry on.' She didn't sound like she believed him, but since he wasn't sure how to convince her, Alex continued with his story.

'So she stumbles out of her house and the driver grabs her case as I help her into the car, and it's then I realise she is sozzled.'

Nell raised her perfectly arched eyebrows. Another beauty point for her. 'Sozzled? She was drunk?'

'Plastered,' Alex said. 'So I guess that was my first clue things weren't going to go so well.'

'What was your second?' She was looking much more amused by this story now, Alex realised.

'Probably when she raided the limo mini-bar.'

Nell snorted at that. 'So by the time you got to the airport…'

'About ready to pass out, or throw up on the steward's shoes. Yes.'

'They wouldn't let her on the plane because she was drunk?' Nell guessed.

'Worse.'

It had been excruciating, trying to steer her through the airport. He had access to the first-class lounge, of course, but Alex hadn't really wanted to take her there. So he'd planned to head to the business class one instead, since they were probably more used to that sort of behaviour, he'd reasoned.

In the event, they hadn't even got that far.

'What happened?' Nell pressed.

'We got stopped at security, and when they searched her bags they found some items that are not entirely legal at the best of times, and definitely not supposed to be taken through airport security.' Alex was almost at the point where he could find this whole story funny, he hoped. If nothing else, it was a good tale to tell at dinner parties.

'Drugs?' Nell looked horrified.

Alex didn't blame her. He liked a drink and he liked fun as much as the next person—when the next person wasn't Nell, who really didn't seem that keen on fun at all, in general. But drugs were not something he'd ever found an attractive prospect. He wouldn't give anything that much control over his character or behaviour.

'Apparently.' He sighed. 'So we spent a significant amount of time with the security team and the police—because obviously they all thought I'd planted them on her.' She'd sobered up remarkably quickly to be able to try and pin the blame on him, really. He'd got lucky in the end that they'd managed to find nothing against him—and more against her, including past drugs charges she'd never mentioned. 'Then eventually they let me go and, well, I'd missed my flight, obviously. And somehow I didn't really fancy New York for the weekend any more.' Or flying anywhere with anyone for a while, really.

'Wow.' Nell stared up at him, eyes wider than ever. 'You know, I think you might be right.'

'Not something I'm used to hearing you say.'

'Yeah, but in this case…your date really *was* worse than mine.' She smiled impishly up at him and Alex couldn't help but laugh in response. Nell tugged on his arm. 'Come on. Time to actually do some work.'

It was only as they turned the last corner back to the office that he realised sharing disastrous date stories with Nell was more fun than any date he'd been on recently.

Even ones that didn't end up with a cavity search.

CHAPTER SIX

THE NEXT WEEKEND was Polly and Fred's engagement party. Nell had tried to argue that it really wasn't appropriate to bring a first date to a family event like this, but Polly had overruled her. So Nell put on her first date dress—black, obviously, but with a wrap top and a split skirt that made it significantly more date-like than her usual work dresses—black block-heeled boots and red lipstick, and waited by the door for tonight's date to show up.

And then she waited some more.

When the message belatedly came through, telling her that her date needed to cancel, it was a relief on two fronts. One, she didn't have to go to the party with a stranger. And two, the knowledge that she'd never be able to date someone who was habitually late, anyway. That would just never work.

She grabbed her black suede jacket, her cross-body bag and her phone and headed out solo.

Polly and the team had commandeered—or at least hired—the gardens and ground floor of a London mansion for the party, one they'd used before with great success. Nell hoped they'd got the same caterers in too. Their crab puffs were to die for…

The venue was tucked away off a moderately palatial London street, with plenty of other similarly impressive houses and buildings along the way. On a normal day it would be impossible to guess which one might be set up as an event venue instead of a family home.

Not so tonight.

Tonight, she could hear the music from across the street, and see the lights almost as soon as she stepped out of the nearest station.

Tonight, the place was alive.

She passed the security guard on the gate easily with a smile—possibly they thought she was Polly, or maybe they actually remembered her from previous events. Either worked.

Guests were being shepherded up the steps, past the columns that fronted the entrance, to where both doors were flung open to welcome them in. Inside the marble floored hall, brightly coloured decorations and balls hung from the ceiling and the bannisters of the double staircase, all the way to the huge glass doors which opened up the whole back of the house onto the garden.

Outside, the flashing lights and music were brighter and louder than ever, and the air was filled with laughter and the odd happy scream as people enjoyed the fairground rides and stalls Polly had arranged for the event.

Nell paused at the bar, set up by the open doors, and grabbed a glass of red wine. It was only then she spotted the lit-up signs welcoming them to the Faire l'Amour. Nell stifled a groan at the title, and wondered how many of the guests would be able to accurately translate it—or plug it into a search engine.

Hopefully not too many.

Another one of Polly's little jokes, she supposed. At first glance, it just looked like a Fair of Love, which, combined with the rides and stalls and the occasion, made perfect sense.

But the *actual* translation…

'Interesting name for tonight, isn't it?' Alex's warm voice spoke close to her ear, easily audible even over all the fairground noise.

She swallowed. Of course *he* knew what it really meant.

'Polly's little joke, I imagine.'

'Oh, I'm sure. Fred was always rubbish in French lessons.'

Nell turned towards him, and swallowed at the sight of him in a dark red V-neck jumper and black jeans. He always looked impeccably good in his suits for work, of course, but she'd become immune to that sight over the years.

Seeing him dressed down, but still immaculately, did things to her insides she didn't care to examine.

After all, this was *Alex McLeod.* He'd always been gorgeous. She'd just learned a long time ago that attractiveness wasn't the same as being someone she could like, trust or rely on not to run out on her after they were getting hot and heavy in his bedroom…

'Probably for the best,' she said, and he looked at her in confusion. It took her a second or two to realise that was because he'd been doing the same thing she was—looking her up and down and getting distracted by her appearance, and now the moment for actually responding to his comment had long passed. She jerked her gaze away and cleared her throat. 'That Fred was rubbish at French, I mean. So he won't translate the signs.'

To make love, that was what it meant.

And suddenly Nell couldn't think about anything else.

What would have happened that night at university, if Fred and the others hadn't interrupted them? If Alex hadn't run out—or if she'd waited for him to get back?

If they hadn't both backed away and avoided each other, embarrassed by what had almost happened between them?

Would they have slept together? Would it have been a one night thing? Would they have tried for something more?

They were too different for her to believe it could have ever lasted between them. But still…the curiosity lingered.

Another couple approached the bar, and Alex put his hand at the small of Nell's back as they moved out of the way and into the garden. He pulled it away as soon as they were outside, but Nell had the strangest feeling she'd have a burned palm print on her skin when she took her dress off later that night.

'So, where's date number two?' Alex asked. 'I was assured you had one for every Saturday night for three months.'

'Stood me up.' Nell gave him an easy smile to show how little she cared. 'So I'm a single rider for the fairground rides tonight.'

'I'm not sure that's allowed.' Alex pointed to a sign printed in bright pink letters, propped up beside what looked like a tunnel of love ride.

Couples only. No single riders.

Of course. Nell sighed. Well, Polly had warned them.

'You'll have to stick with me.' There was something in his voice that made Polly turn towards him, studying his face as she tried to put her finger on what it was.

'Where's *your* date?' she asked, still unsure as to what the strange dynamic between them tonight added up to. 'Don't tell me she's stuck at Customs.'

He laughed, low and hot. 'Not tonight. Tonight, she ran into her ex—who also hadn't got the memo about couples only and had shown up stag. They got talking and, well, when I spotted you at the bar and made my escape I'm not sure either of them even noticed.'

He told the story nonchalantly enough but Nell winced on his behalf, anyway. Maybe for him it was just another story to tell at parties, but she knew if it had been her she'd have run away and hidden for the rest of the night.

Not Alex, though. 'Come on,' he said, tugging on her arm. 'Let's go find some rides to go on before we get stuck into the doughnuts and candy floss.'

Glad she'd worn her boots, she followed him out onto the dewy spring grass towards the rides—and then stopped stock-still as she spotted a familiar face in the queue for the carousel.

Alex made it a step forward before falling back again, following her stare. 'Is that…'

'Yes.'

'Paul?'

'Yes.'

'What's he doing here?' There was a hint of anger in Alex's voice, presumably on Nell's behalf, which she appreciated.

'I have absolutely zero idea,' she admitted.

Why on earth would Polly have invited Nell's ex-boyfriend to her engagement party?

Unless…

'Who is that he's standing with?' she asked, her voice small.

Couples only, that was the rule. Which meant he must be here with another woman.

The woman he'd left her for.

The one he'd told her was more exciting. More fun.

Who made him feel more alive than he'd ever felt with Nell.

The one he'd probably been *faire l'amour*-ing with while they were still living together.

'Oh,' Alex said in the sort of tone that told her she wasn't going to like the answer to that question. 'That's Fred's cousin, Jemima. I didn't realise *she* was…'

'The one he left me for. Apparently.'

Over in the queue, Jemima flipped her long, perfectly highlighted and waved hair over her shoulder and smiled adoringly up at the man Nell had expected to marry.

'Shall we go find Polly and Fred?' Alex asked gently. He must think her so pathetic. Broken, even.

But she wasn't. Not even close.

It would take a lot more than a cheating boyfriend to break her.

Nell stared at Paul and Jemima for one more moment, then turned away. 'No. We came to the fair. I want to go on some rides then eat enough doughnuts to make me sick.'

'Okay then,' Alex replied, taking her arm as he had done in the park earlier that week. 'Then let's go find us a ride.'

Nell vetoed the Ferris wheel out of hand.

'What if it gets stuck?' she asked incredulously when he suggested it.

'Is this because of your lift date?' Alex enjoyed the way her cheeks turned a little pink at the suggestion. 'Because not everything that goes up in the air gets stuck, you realise.'

'I don't like heights,' she admitted. 'And getting stuck at the top of one of those things...' She shuddered and Alex wrapped an arm around her shoulders instinctively. 'It's basically one of my recurring nightmares.'

'No Ferris wheel, then.' Alex steered her away, scanning the fairground for another ride she might enjoy.

It wasn't a *real* fairground, of course—there wasn't quite the space for that, even in the palatial grounds of the London house Polly had hired. Not unless the owners were willing to sacrifice a few trees and shrubs, anyway, which Alex suspected they weren't.

In addition to the Ferris wheel there was the carousel—where Paul and Jemima were currently queuing, so that was out; the dodgems, except Alex worried Nell might be a little too susceptible to road rage given her current state of mind; a ride that seemed to go up into the air then plummet to the ground, which was probably worse than the Ferris wheel and…

Oh, of course.

'Tunnel of Love it is, then,' he told her, changing their course.

There was a small queue so they waited their turn, and Alex took the opportunity to take in the sights and sounds of the fairground. It wasn't quite the real thing, he knew that. But it was still the closest he'd ever got to it.

'There used to be a fair that came to the village nearest our estate most summers,' he told Nell. He wasn't sure why, exactly, except that she looked like she needed the distraction tonight, and telling stories about his life was sort of his default for that.

Usually they were stories that made him sound adventurous, stories filled with drama—or ones that made people laugh, and think he was a good sport.

This wasn't any of those, but then, Nell wasn't his usual audience either.

'I'd look out of my bedroom window at the lights, and listen to the screams and the laughter,' he went on. 'Sometimes I could even smell the frying doughnuts on the breeze. God, I would have given *anything* to go down to the fair.'

He hadn't been totally sure she was even listening, but now she looked at him in surprise. 'You never went?'

Alex shrugged. 'It wasn't an appropriate place for Callum McLeod's son to be seen.'

Was that pity in her eyes? Alex hoped not. There was nothing anyone should pity him for. He'd grown up rich, privileged and wanting for nothing—except possibly a night at the fair.

He knew how lucky he was.

The Tunnel of Love didn't look quite like the ones he'd seen in the movies—probably because this was a small ride that had to be transported around the country. As such, the swan boats that journeyed through the short tunnel travelled on rails, rather than bobbing along on water.

Still, he thought as he helped Nell inside and she tucked her skirt around her legs to stop him sitting on it, the basics were the same. A couple pressed up close together in a small, romantic boat, travelling through a dark space where anything could happen…

Nell flashed him a look as the swan started to move. 'Don't go getting any ideas, now.'

'Wouldn't dream of it,' Alex lied.

The ideas were already there. Had been for years—since the last time he'd kissed her, and returned to his room to find her gone.

And it was hard not to imagine kissing Nell as she laughed at the ridiculous lit-up cupids and glow-in-the-dark hearts that filled the tunnel.

'Only Polly would think something like this is romantic,' she explained when he looked at her. 'All this… For Polly, romance is something you have to show, perform even.'

'She wears her heart on her sleeve,' Alex

agreed cautiously. 'She doesn't hide how she feels.' Unlike her sister, he suspected.

'Never mind her sleeve—her heart has a permanent megaphone attached.' Nell sighed. 'I love her dearly, but sometimes I wonder how we came from the same womb.'

Since Alex had been wondering the same thing, he just nodded.

The swan boat jerked around a corner and Nell was jostled closer into his side. Alex wrapped an arm around her instinctively and, when she didn't shrug it off, kept it there.

'Why do you think you *are* so different?' he asked.

Nell looked up at his question, her skin taking on a pinkish tinge from the lights inside the tunnel. 'I don't know. Well, I guess I do.'

She just didn't want to talk about it, Alex read between the lines. But the way she worried her bottom lip with her teeth just thinking about it suggested to him that maybe she needed to.

So he pushed. 'Tell me.'

'When we were growing up… I always knew that, as much as we looked the same, Polly and I were different inside. That's just how we were born. But maybe it was also, well, encouraged by the different ways we reacted to our upbringing.'

'How do you mean?' Polly didn't talk much about her family and, to his knowledge, Nell never did. All he knew was that their father had died when they were very young, and they'd spent a lot of time with their grandparents after that. 'You mean your dad?'

'Partly. I mean, it's not like we saw a lot of him *before* he died. He was an adventurer, did you know that?' She pulled a face. 'As if that has ever been a real job.'

'Polly told me he was a treasure-hunter once,' Alex remembered suddenly. 'Diving old shipwrecks and the like, looking for booty?'

'That's the one.' There was a sour note in Nell's voice he didn't quite understand.

'That's...pretty cool, isn't it?'

She shot him a look. 'What? Flying around the world to search for treasure nobody has wanted or needed for decades, or even hundreds of years, instead of, oh, I don't know, staying and raising your daughters?'

Ah. Put that way, Alex supposed it *wasn't* all that cool.

'We didn't see him for months at a time—even a year once. It was hard to tell the difference, really, when he died searching that wreck.' The lines at the corner of her mouth said otherwise. As much as Alex believed

Nell *wished* she didn't care, he suspected that in truth she cared far too much. He wondered how many other things that was true about, and he'd just never noticed before.

'I'm sorry,' he murmured.

'He just left us with *her*. Except she wasn't all that interested either.'

'Your mother?'

'Yeah.' She looked away, even as the swan cornered the last bend at a slight angle, pressing her closer against his side.

Alex thought about his own parents. About his father, locked away in their castle on the hill, the latest in a long line of McLeod men who'd stayed put, however miserable they got. About his mother, storming in and out with her temper and the wind. And about the boy he'd been, growing up looking out at a world that never seemed accessible to him—until he'd finally left for boarding school and discovered it had just been waiting for him to arrive.

'Polly always was more like her, really,' Nell said softly. 'She had her charm. I never did.'

'I don't know about that,' Alex said, his own voice low and almost lost in the crunch of the swan coming to a halt at the end of the ride.

Nell's smile was sad. 'Everyone else does.' She hopped out of the swan and held a hand out to pull him up too. 'Come on. I think it's time for doughnuts. Don't you?'

CHAPTER SEVEN

POLLY WAS OVERFLOWING with apologies about Paul's presence at the party, when they finally caught up.

'I had no idea she was bringing *him,*' she promised. 'I'd have said no if I had!'

'How could you?' Nell asked. 'I mean, she's Fred's cousin and he's her boyfriend.'

'Yeah, but you're my sister and he's your *ex*-boyfriend.' Polly's arms were folded tightly across her chest. 'I've already told Fred she can't bring him to the wedding.'

'Except then she won't have a pair, for all the couple stuff,' Nell pointed out. 'So unless you're going to uninvite Fred's cousin…'

A frown line settled between Polly's eyebrows. 'If I have to.'

Nell sighed. 'No. Don't do that. I don't want to make a big deal about it, have Jemima cause a scene or anything. Just…don't seat them near me at the wedding breakfast, okay?'

'Are you sure?' Polly asked, and Nell nodded. 'Okay, then. But they're definitely not coming to the stag and hen do, though.'

'Agreed.'

Nell had hoped that being the reasonable one, and not making a big deal about her ex being at the wedding, would buy her some time in Polly's good graces. Time that might be spent not having to continue her search for her own date for the big day.

But the goodwill her magnanimity bought her didn't last anywhere near long enough for Nell's liking.

'You're running out of time, you realise.' Polly's voice was arch and when Nell looked up from her computer screen she saw her twin leaning against her doorway, eyebrows raised and knowing smile in place. 'A girl might think that you'd abandoned the idea of finding anyone other than Alex McLeod to go to my wedding with after all.'

'I have another date tomorrow night.' Nell tried to sound rather more enthusiastic about that than she felt. 'One of these set-ups has to actually go well eventually, right?'

'If you let them,' Polly replied, before drifting away, back downstairs to where the action happened. 'Just let me know what name to put on the seating plan,' she called back over her shoulder.

Nell tried to turn her attention back to the numbers on the spreadsheet that filled her screen, but they all seemed to blur to one. Instead, so dropped her head in her hands and wondered how she'd ended up here.

Probably it was Polly's fault. This sort of thing usually was.

The worst part was she'd been doing exactly as they'd planned. She'd been on a damn date every single Saturday night for the past month, since her no-show at the engagement party. And every one had been an unmitigated disaster.

Polly thought she was sabotaging them. Her reasoning seemed to vacillate between believing that Nell was still hung up on Paul—whose relationship with the perfect Jemima seemed to be going from strength to strength, damn him—thinking that she was just trying to prove some point to Polly, or suspecting that Nell really did want to go to the wedding with Alex after all.

All of which was nonsense. Especially the last one.

Okay, maybe they'd shared a moment riding that stupid swan at Polly and Fred's engagement party.

And maybe the best part about all her stupid dating site set-ups was sharing how awful they were with Alex over coffee in the park on a Monday morning, while he told his own horror stories about his attempts to find a date for the wedding.

She sat back in her chair and smiled as she remembered all those Monday mornings. As the daffodils had faded and the first summer blooms had begun to appear, they'd shared tales from dating hell and laughed so much that even the most excruciatingly embarrassing stories didn't seem quite so bad any more.

Like the riverboat cruise down the Seine with the man who'd whisked her away to Paris. As the water had started coming in from the sides and they'd all been evacuated in blow-up boats, she'd thought that Alex would never be able to top that one.

Then it turned out his date had stolen his car.

Week after week, failed date after failed date. And Monday morning coffee with Alex was the only bright spot in the whole endeavour.

But that didn't have to mean anything. Did it?

She was sure it wouldn't to him. It hadn't last time, after all.

And she wasn't about to make the same mistake again, that was certain.

Her date the next night was 'a surprise'—which meant the guy was already off to a bad start, as surely Polly must have put in her profile how much she hated surprises.

All the same, Nell slipped into a black wrap dress and tall boots, opting for her leather jacket on top this time, and headed out to meet him on the South Bank. At least it was far enough from St Pancras station that there was little chance he was going to take her on another waterlogged adventure in Paris.

One of these dates has to stick, she reminded herself as she hurried to meet the guy.

If it didn't, her only option would be to succumb to being Alex's pity date for the wedding, and she couldn't face that—even if, after the last month or two, she suspected they'd actually have fun together.

That wasn't the point.

The point was…

What was the point again?

She recognised the man leaning against the railing by the Thames from his photo on the dating site and headed towards him, still trying to order her thoughts. He was dark-haired, tall, handsome…and he reminded her just a little too much of Alex.

Not that she was thinking about Alex tonight. Except about how she didn't want to be his date for the wedding.

Because she was better than a pity date, that was the point. Alex would take her, she was almost certain, because it turned out he'd grown up into a nicer guy than she'd expected. And they had more fun together than she suspected either of them would have predicted.

But it wasn't the real thing. Neither of them thought for a moment that the pair of them made sense together. He was all about adventures and drama and tall tales. And she was very much not.

She wanted a guy who'd stay home and live a quiet, boring life with her. The sort of life she'd imagined she could have with Paul.

And that just wasn't how Alex lived his life.

They'd both known what a bad fit they were for each other back at university, when they'd swerved to avoid a train wreck between them before it ever really happened. Yeah, she'd been mad at him for walking out when things were just getting interesting between them, but after that had faded she knew he'd made the right choice. They just didn't match up, so better not to try.

Nothing had changed in the years since then to make that equation add up now.

Everyone at the wedding would know they weren't really together. That Alex had taken pity on her and paired up with her rather than bringing his own date. And she couldn't bear people talking about her like that.

So, she'd better hope this guy was the one.

Pasting on a smile, she marched over to the railings and introduced herself.

Her date, Richard, returned her smile with a warm one of his own, and even instigated a hug hello. He seemed charming, and unlikely to have a panic attack in a lift or book a boat with holes in it.

And, up close, he hardly looked like Alex at all.

This could work.

'So, what's the plan for tonight?' she asked, still smiling.

'Have you ever been on the London Eye?' Richard asked, and Nell felt her stomach sink.

Richard had paid for some sort of special ticket that meant they didn't have to queue at all, and they had their pod almost entirely to themselves—just a few other couples. There was a table set up in the middle, laden with champagne and chocolate-dipped strawberries, and waiting staff to serve them. Really, it was all very romantic and thoughtful.

Nell made her way to the edge, step by shuffling step, and held on for dear life to the railing that ran around the pod.

Everything is glassed in. It's perfectly safe. What's the worst that could happen?

She heard voices behind her as the last couple was admitted to the pod, but she focused on Richard standing beside her, rather than their companions.

The pod moved slowly, slowly upwards.

It wasn't really like a Ferris wheel at all, Nell reassured herself. It didn't spin, or race around. It wasn't even a ride. It was a tourist attraction, designed to showcase London in all its glory.

At night, the lights of the city were mesmerising. Nell focused on staring outwards, far over the river, listening to Richard lecturing her about everything they could see—or couldn't, since it was night-time. Not very much of it went in, but then she'd lived in London her whole life. It wasn't as if she didn't already know where things were.

Her stomach dropped a little as they reached the top, but at least that meant she was closer to the end than the beginning, didn't it? Richard had gone quiet—perhaps intuiting that she wasn't actually listening to him at all. But she'd be more fun once they got off the wheel of death. Not a lot more fun, admittedly. But maybe enough that they could get a nice dinner together.

This was all going to be okay.

Then the Eye jerked, shuddered…

And stopped in mid-air.

Alex had recognised Nell the moment he and his date stepped onto the London Eye. No one else had that shimmering black hair combined with that defensive, determined stance as she stood staring out over London.

She hates heights, and has a fear of Ferris wheels. What idiot would bring her here for her first date?

The idiot, he reasoned, must be the man standing beside her.

Another Saturday, another date from that damned dating site.

For his own date, he'd brought a friend of a friend of a friend. Mollie—his actual friend—had been trying to persuade him to listen to her advice on who to date for years. She'd been thrilled when he'd finally taken her up on the offer. And he'd been pretty pleased with the situation when he'd picked up Eva for the evening too. She was blonde, beautiful and not high, drunk or likely to steal his car.

That made her a winner by his current, admittedly low standards.

Eva tucked her arm through his and tugged him over to the far side of the pod as they started to move.

'So, are you going to tell me all the things we can see?' she asked with an indulgent smile. As if that was what people did on dates on the London Eye.

Maybe it was. Alex had never brought anyone here before.

He looked out at the pitch-black London night sky, dotted with lights of buildings, planes and stars, the lit-up landmarks he could make out so obvious that no Londoner would need them naming. Then he glanced back at her and shrugged. 'It's night-time. You can't see much of anything. Champagne?'

On the other side of the pod, Nell's knuckles were white as she clutched the railings. Alex could see them, bone-white, even at a distance.

'God, she has to be hating this.'

'Who?' Eva looked up at him in confusion. 'Hating what?'

Alex nodded towards Nell. 'That's a...

friend of mine. She doesn't like heights. Or Ferris wheels.'

'Then why on earth did she come on here?' Eva asked.

'So she wouldn't have to go to a wedding with me.'

Nell's date had stopped prattling on in her ear and had taken a step aside. Alex was just wondering if he should go over, let her know he was there and check she was okay, when the whole Eye shuddered to a halt.

With their pod right at the top.

This is literally her worst nightmare.

Okay, so it wasn't quite like being stuck at the top of a Ferris wheel, like she'd told him she feared. The London Eye pods were all enclosed, and they were wandering around drinking champagne and eating chocolate-dipped strawberries, rather than dangling exposed from a rickety metal chair.

But if we were on a Ferris wheel, I could put my arm around her like I did on the swan boat in the Tunnel of Love. I could keep her safe.

Right now, she didn't even know he was here.

'If you want to go look after your friend, that's okay,' Eva said, sounding genuinely amused. 'I'm sure there are plenty of other people here who can explain the London skyline in the dark to me.'

She was already eyeing up Nell's wandering date, he realised. Well, good luck to them both. With a nod to Eva, he headed over to Nell, making sure she saw him, knew he was here, before he settled an arm around her shivering shoulders.

'Okay?' he murmured softly.

'Of course I'm okay. Why wouldn't I be?' The sharpness in her voice was fear, he realised, rather than disdain. But if he hadn't known about her Ferris wheel nightmare, he'd have assumed the latter.

How many other times in the past had he done that? Taken Nell's defensiveness as dismissal, rather than vulnerability?

Probably too many.

Like that night at university when he'd kissed her, then been dragged away—and she'd been gone when he returned. He'd always assumed her coldness towards him after that night was because she'd realised what she'd almost done while drunk and hated him for taking advantage of her that way.

But what if it was something else…?

He shook his head. That train of thought was going to lead him away from what Nell needed from him tonight, which was, he guessed, distraction.

'Apparently the done thing on a night date on the London Eye is to describe the skyline we can't actually see very well. Would you like me to try?'

That earned him a laugh, at least. 'Richard has already done that, thanks. I wasn't really listening though.'

Alex glanced back across the pod to another two heads, pressed close together, looking out over the skyline. 'And now I believe he's telling Eva. My date.'

'How romantic,' Nell said drily. 'Guess this is another failed date for the books.'

'Oh, I don't know. It doesn't seem to be going so badly for Richard and Eva.'

'True.'

They both stared out through the glass of the pod as they waited for it to start moving again. It didn't.

'Why do you date such boring men, anyway?' Alex asked, already anticipating the glare she would send his way. If she was angry she wasn't scared and, in his book at least, that was an improvement.

'Boring is all a state of mind,' she retorted. 'I prefer to think of my preferred sort of date as stable, reliable and reassuring. All things this piece of steel and glass isn't.' Her glare was redirected to the centre of the London Eye.

'Still. Don't you ever want a little more adventure?' He waggled his eyebrows to try and make her laugh. 'I mean, as long as it doesn't end with you stuck in the air in a confined space, or sinking on the Seine?'

Nell didn't laugh. 'You're thinking of my parents, or Polly. They're the adrenaline junkies, remember?'

'And you have to be contrary because you can't want what they want?' He'd started this conversation as a distraction, but now Alex found himself invested in the answers.

'No. Because I'm a different sort of person to them. And I don't think love is what *they* think it is.' A waiter passed with a tray, and she grabbed a glass of champagne and practically downed it in one. Belatedly, Alex reached for one of his own—only for Nell to take that one from him too.

At least she didn't down that one. But he suspected the situation was getting to her rather more than she'd admit.

'What do they think love is?' he asked.

Nell shrugged. '*You* know. All drama and tension and arguing and making up and running away and coming back. High romance and drama.'

'You mean passion,' he replied. 'There's nothing wrong with some real passion between people who care about each other.'

His own parents were proof of that. His mother might leave, but she always came back.

They had passion. That was the important thing. If they didn't fight and make up, how would anyone know they loved each other?

'Passion?' Nell shook her head. 'That's not passion. That's drama. It's just that some people prefer that to the real thing.'

'People like Polly and Fred?' he asked, mostly to distract himself now from the fact he'd always thought passion and drama *were* the same thing.

Well, what did he know? At least one ex-girlfriend had told him he'd never know real love if it slapped him in the face. Maybe they were right.

Nell's expression softened at the mention of her sister. 'No, Polly and Fred are the real thing. They just like the drama too.' She frowned for a moment, and when she spoke again it was with the surprise of realisation in her voice. 'I guess maybe it's possible to have both.'

'Maybe,' Alex agreed. 'Or maybe you and I know nothing about love.'

Finally, that got him the laugh he'd been angling for. And as it echoed off the glass of the pod, the wheel finally started turning again, resulting in a loud cheer going up from all the people in it.

'Would you want to?' Nell asked, her tone serious again.

'Want to what?'

'Know about love?'

Alex didn't have to think about his answer. 'Doesn't everybody?'

'I suppose so,' Nell said thoughtfully.

He just wondered if either of them ever would.

CHAPTER EIGHT

HAVING SPENT THEIR Saturday night together, stuck at the top of the London Eye, there was no real need for a Monday morning debrief over coffee—which meant that Nell and Alex both made it to the Start the Week staff meeting early for a change.

'So?' Polly asked as they took their seats. 'How were your respective dates this weekend?'

Nell glanced over at Alex, who was already looking at her.

'Safe to say, I don't think either of us are planning to bring our Saturday night dates to the wedding,' he said drily.

Fred gave them both a sympathetic look. 'That bad?'

'Mine took me up the London Eye,' Nell explained. 'And it got stuck.'

Polly winced. 'Not ideal.'

'No.' She sneaked another look at Alex. 'Luckily Alex was there to talk me down.'

'Oh?' Polly hopped to the edge of her seat, leaning her elbows on the table as she looked between them. 'How come?'

Alex lifted one shoulder in a casual shrug. 'The London Eye's a classic, right? I just happened to be there with my date too. I knew Nell doesn't like heights or big wheels, so… Anyway, my date was more interested in *her* date's explanation of the London skyline. It all worked out.' Another shrug, which somehow had the effect of making his laidback sprawl in his chair look less casual.

Polly narrowed her eyes. 'So it was just a coincidence?'

'Completely,' Nell assured her. The last thing she needed was her sister getting ideas at this point.

'Or fate.' Polly's lips twisted up in an amused grin. 'I'm definitely putting my money on fate.'

'And I'm putting mine on us running out of ways to have lousy dates every weekend, just to fulfil your couples only wedding nightmare.' It was cruel, and she regretted the words almost the moment they were out of her mouth—and definitely by the time the hurt showed on Polly's face.

Fred, ever the peacemaker, stepped in.

'Don't worry, Nell,' he said in an earnestly reassuring voice. 'I'm sure you and Alex will both be able to find a date at the stag and hen do—someone who's already coming to the wedding anyway would be perfect, right? And Pol did say you needed a date by the *end* of the stag and hen weekend. Besides, there's bound to be plenty of people you both know.'

'People we haven't already dated?' Nell asked caustically, thinking of Paul and Jemima at the engagement party fairground.

'That's a thought.' Fred turned to Alex. 'I think Caitlin is going to be there, Alex, and I'm not sure she's said who she's bringing yet.'

Caitlin, Nell's foggy memory reminded her, was Alex's last but one semi-serious girlfriend, who had left him high and dry after walking out of another wedding four years ago, when Alex had been best man. They'd had a huge argument in the vestry before the service, as she recalled. One that every single guest in the church heard every word of, until the organist stepped it up a notch.

Always with the drama, these people.

Alex wasn't keen on the idea of a reunion anyway, if the sour look on his face was any indication.

And neither, it seemed, was Polly. 'Fred! He's not dating Caitlin again.' Nell imagined she remembered what had happened last time too. Not what she'd been hoping for at her own festival of romance wedding.

Fred gave her a confused look. 'But I thought we were *supposed* to be helping them find dates.'

'Not that one,' Polly replied shortly.

But someone. The idea that Alex *wouldn't* find someone to take to the wedding, even in the now shortened timeframe they had left, was laughable.

'Well, at least we know someone he's dated before is someone he's attracted to,' Fred pointed out. 'And we know he *really* doesn't want to go with Nell!'

Fred—good old slightly oblivious Fred—laughed. Then stopped when he realised no one else was.

The slight burn at the back of her throat, the sting in her eyes…they weren't caused by tears, Nell told herself. Because why would she want to cry at that? Fred was absolutely right. Alex really *didn't* want to go to the wedding with Nell—and she didn't want to go with him either. She didn't even want him to *want* to go with her, because she wasn't the kind of person who enjoyed that kind of drama power trip.

Alex didn't want her now, any more than

he'd really wanted her when they were back at university. And she was fine with that.

She just wanted to find a date for this wedding, and so did he. And maybe Fred was right, and the hen and stag party was their best shot at doing that.

They should both be open to that possibility. Encourage it even.

And she really, really needed to stop remembering that moment on the London Eye, when she'd felt like all she could do was curl up in a ball and cry, until Alex had come over and distracted her from her fear.

She wasn't going to think about how he'd known instinctively exactly what she'd needed. Or even the fact that he'd remembered about her fears at all.

It didn't mean anything after all. Just that Alex McLeod was more of a decent human being than she'd always assumed.

Nell pushed her chair away from the table and stalked to the door. 'I assume we're done here?'

They hadn't actually talked about work, she realised. But apparently everyone realised that they weren't going to, because nobody tried to stop her.

She considered stopping by the kitchen for a coffee, but decided she couldn't face the chatter and the gossip. So instead she headed straight for the narrow stairs that led to her attic office, and prepared to spend her day dealing with numbers rather than people.

They made much more sense, in her experience.

And her spreadsheets wouldn't ask her why, if she didn't want to go to the wedding with Alex McLeod, she kept thinking about that night on the Eye together, or their evening at the fairground, and remembering how much more like a date they'd felt than any of the set-ups she'd been on through the dating agency.

If she got really lucky, her spreadsheets and numbers might even distract her from the fact that she'd liked that feeling.

A lot more than she'd meant to.

When Polly and Fred had asked if it would be possible to hold the joint stag and hen party at his family estate in Scotland, Alex hadn't been able to find a reason to say no.

Well, actually, he'd had a hundred reasons ready to go. But none that weren't horribly selfish, or required a lot more conversation about his childhood and his relationship with his parents than he was willing to enter into.

Which meant that, in the end, he'd said yes.

And now teams of Here & Now staff were descending on his family home, setting up what was sure to be the party of the year.

'Are those hot-air balloons, darling?' His mother stood beside him, peering out of the window at the industrious activity going on across the West Lawn.

'Apparently so.' Alex had tried to persuade his parents that they might prefer to be somewhere else this weekend, but to no avail.

'Nonsense!' his father had said. 'We love a good party as much as the next person, don't we, Shelly?' His mother had, of course, agreed.

And Alex had given up.

Because he knew it wasn't just the party his parents loved. It was the noise and the drama, and they never could stop themselves getting swept up in it.

Ah, well. His mother hadn't stomped out of High Dudgeon House—as it had been nicknamed by Fred when he came to stay one summer in their teens—for at least eighteen months. She was probably due.

And he'd spend the next few months reminding them both how much they actually loved each other, and him, and the life they had together, until she floated back in and they were sickeningly adoring again—until the next time.

He'd been through this far too often to expect them to stray from the formula this weekend. So he just steeled himself for the inevitability, and reminded himself that this was how his parents showed their love. It was demonstrative, over-the-top and, yes, time-consuming for him. But they were still together, after all these years, despite everything.

This was love. Passion. Drama. Just like in the movies.

Who was he to argue with that? Even if he didn't want it for himself.

Fred and Polly subscribed to the same show-your-love-with-excess school of thought as his parents, although hopefully without the breakups and makeups. Which was why there was now a small fleet of hot-air balloons scattered across the West Lawn and the fields beyond.

Who threw a party in hot-air balloons?

Alex pitied the poor DJ, who had to make the music work across all the balloons. Not to mention the balloon operators—were they called pilots? He should ask, it would be polite—who would have to deal with all the partygoers. Alex knew most of them. That wouldn't be easy.

In fact, as best man, he really should be helping.

Making his excuses to his mother—who declared she needed to go and get ready for the party anyway—Alex made his way outside to see how things were going.

'Ah, there you are!' Polly beckoned him over with expansive gestures. 'I know we said you wouldn't have to do much as best man—'

'Except let us use this magnificent venue,' Fred interjected, and Polly acknowledged the point with a nod.

'But we did rather hope you'd actually be here,' she finished. 'Where have you been hiding?'

'Just paying my respects to the parentals,' Alex explained.

Fred pulled a sympathetic face. 'And how are they?'

'Looking about ready to pull their latest greatest drama,' Alex admitted. 'Don't worry, I'll try and keep it off-stage for your party, at least.'

'It would be appreciated,' Polly said drily. 'I would rather like my wedding events to be more about Fred and me than your parents' drawn-out foreplay habit.'

Alex winced at the description, but he had to admit she had a point. 'It's romantic? In a way?'

Polly gave him a look. 'If that's what you think romance looks like, no wonder you haven't got a date to our wedding yet.'

Alex thought back to his discussions about love with Nell on the London Eye. 'Your sister said something similar the other night.'

'Where is the maid of honour, anyway?' Fred asked. Polly looked to Alex for an answer, and he shrugged.

'Why would I know?'

'No reason,' Polly said airily. 'I just thought… Anyway, she texted me earlier. Her train was delayed.'

'Why didn't she fly up here like everyone else?' Fred's brow was furrowed in confusion.

'Afraid of heights. And flying,' Alex said absently, and shrugged when Fred gave him a strange look. 'We've spent time together.' Enough that he suspected Nell's delay might have more to do with hoping to miss the hot-air balloon ride at the start of the party than anything else.

'I noticed.' Polly's eyes narrowed. 'Well, as part of your best man duties, I'm putting you in charge of the maid of honour for the evening, okay? I'm going to be too busy with my guests.'

Alex raised an eyebrow. 'Are you under the illusion that *you* have been in charge of Nell before now?' From his own observations, it most often seemed the other way around. Nell tempered Polly's flighty enthusiasm, brought her down to earth when she threatened to fly away. Although he supposed Fred had taken on more of those responsibilities over recent years.

Still, it was impossible to imagine *any-one* taking charge of Nell. She was her own woman—and a competent, brilliant one at that. She didn't need looking after that way.

Polly flapped a hand at him. 'Oh, you know what I mean! Just make sure she doesn't freak out too much about the balloons.' Her expression turned suddenly sly. 'You seemed to do a good job of distracting her on the London Eye, after all.'

Before Alex could question what she meant by that, Polly had already dragged Fred away, towards the largest of the hot-air balloons in the centre of the lawn. The other assembled guests, having been shown to their rooms earlier and given the opportunity to change into their finest evening gowns and dinner jackets, were now being herded towards the balloon baskets—or lured in by the trays of champagne that awaited them.

Alex had to admit that the sight as the balloons started to take flight was spectacular.

The sun just starting to sink behind the mountains, the sky filling with brightly coloured hot-air balloons, the music playing magically between all of them—including the one still on the ground, waiting for the last few guests.

Polly might have gone over the top with her wedding plans, but she'd definitely proved that Here & Now knew how to put on a show. Alex predicted a whole rush of hot-air balloon parties on their books next year.

He turned back towards the house and saw a figure running down the path towards him. *Nell.* Her dark evening gown billowed out behind her, revealing the boots she was wearing underneath. Her silky black hair streamed out over her shoulders in the early evening breeze as she clutched a camel-coloured wrap around her.

He could see the flush of pink on her cheeks before he could make out the brightness of her blue eyes, and he knew—somewhere deep in his gut that he usually tried to ignore—that he was in trouble tonight.

Not because she was so beautiful. Not because of the romance of the night. Not even because she was here, in his homeland.

But because she was Nell. And it turned out that meant so much more than he'd ever realised back at university, or in any of the years since.

She finally reached him, and smiled—and Alex felt his heart contract.

'Did I miss the balloon part?' Nell asked hopefully.

'No such luck, I'm afraid.' Alex reached out a hand to her, and she took it. 'There's one balloon waiting just for us. Come on.' She hesitated, and he felt her pulse of fear. 'You can keep holding my hand if you're scared.'

She straightened her shoulders at that. 'Of course I'm not scared,' she said, even though they both knew it was a lie. 'Come on.'

Nell stalked towards the last balloon with a look of grim determination on her face.

But she didn't let go of his hand.

CHAPTER NINE

OBJECTIVELY, NELL HAD to admit that the view from the hot-air balloon was gorgeous. She felt as if she were floating, weightless, in the early evening air as the sun started to set.

Somehow, Polly had managed to get classical music piped into each of the baskets, and the melody lulled her as she looked out over the rolling hills, lochs and the roof of Alex's home castle.

In fact, the views and the music—and the champagne—were almost enough to help her forget her fear of heights, or all the ways she could die horribly if something went wrong with the balloon.

But they still weren't enough to distract her from the heaviness in the air between her and Alex, or the way she could sense every tiny movement he made, as if he were touching her, even when he was keeping what distance it was possible to keep in a balloon basket.

She recognised that feeling. Remembered how it had ended last time too.

What would make this time any different?

'How are you doing?' Alex's voice was low and rumbly in her ear, only just audible over the noise of the balloon and the music. He still wasn't touching her, though—even if all the hairs on her arms stood up in anticipation of it.

'Finding it hard to believe that you grew up in an actual castle,' she admitted. 'I know you always said it was, but...well, the crenellations were a bit of a surprise.'

He chuckled at that. 'It's something, that's for sure. You know Fred calls it High Dudgeon House?'

'Why is that?' She'd always assumed it was just another of those inside jokes that Alex, Fred and Polly shared—and that she'd always be on the outside of. She'd grown used to those over the years, as she'd pulled back from them.

'Because my mother has a tendency to storm out of there in a high dudgeon, as we call it. Then it takes a lot of expensive gifts and humiliating begging when she returns—or on my father's part to get her to come back in the first place. Once he's decided to forgive her, anyway.'

'Sounds exhausting,' Nell said. Like dealing with her own mother, in lots of ways.

'It is.'

The balloon banked a little to the right, and Nell stumbled a little as she tried to find her footing. But suddenly there were strong arms around her middle, and the scent of Alex—clean and fresh and just a little bit spicy—surrounded her too.

She swallowed, hard, when he didn't let go.

'Did you know, the pilot has practically no control at all over where the balloon goes, or where it lands,' she said. 'I was reading up on hot-air balloon rides on the train up.'

'Of course you were,' Alex murmured. Then he raised his voice, and she felt him turn his head towards their pilot. 'Is that true?'

The pilot hummed agreement. Really, Alex should just trust her research skills.

'He just has to look for a suitable field, when we get closer to landing time,' she went on. 'Polly's arranged for four-by-fours to meet us wherever we land—I guess they're following us now—and drive us back to the house for dinner.'

'As long as we don't drift off McLeod land, we should be fine,' Alex mused. Nell twisted her neck to give him a questioning look.

'We've got a decades-old feud going with the neighbours.'

'Of course you have.' More drama. Naturally.

Alex laughed. 'What's that supposed to mean?'

'That just seems to be your life—all high emotion and drama.'

'But not yours?'

She shrugged. 'I like the quiet life.'

'Always?' The question in his voice seemed somehow more meaningful than the word suggested.

'As a rule,' she said casually.

But she was hyperaware of his arms, still wrapped tight around her waist, and the way her body responded to his closeness. A moment like this, with a man she had, until recently, if not despised, certainly avoided as being the opposite of everything she wanted in her life—she had to admit there was a certain drama to it.

Especially since they were flying in a private hot-air balloon above his family's country estate.

This wasn't quiet. This wasn't boring.

This was so far out of her comfort zone she didn't even know how to get back.

'Does this feel quiet to you?' His whisper

seemed to bypass her brain and go straight to her nerve-endings, setting everything tingling.

'No,' she admitted, her voice hoarse.

'Me neither.'

That surprised her—enough that she turned in his arms, leaving the view behind her and focusing on his face instead.

There, deep in his eyes, she saw something she hadn't expected. Something she felt reflected inside herself.

Heat.

Not just the gentle warmth of familiarity or fondness she was used to feeling with Paul or any of her other ex-boyfriends.

This was something different. Something new. Or something old, perhaps. Something she hadn't felt since the night she ran away from his room at university.

Something she thought might burn her up from the inside and leave her a different person altogether.

Would it burn away her fear? Or just leave her more things to be afraid of?

Nell didn't know.

But in that moment she wasn't sure she cared either.

She'd spent all her life trying to avoid the kind of drama her mother courted, the sort of high emotion that had made her childhood such a misery. She knew that wasn't a life she wanted for herself—or any children she might have herself, one day.

She wasn't the same sort of person as the rest of her family—or as Alex and his family either.

But maybe, just this once, she wanted a taste of how that passion felt. For real, this time.

A taste that wouldn't leave her wondering for years again afterwards.

'Nell,' Alex said, and she could hear the restraint in his voice. He was holding himself back, from her. *For* her.

Because this was madness—they both knew that. It would be hard to find a less compatible pair than the woman who wanted to stay home every Friday night in her slippers and the man who thought nothing of inviting a woman he'd only met once to New York for the weekend for a first date.

But tonight—here and now, drifting over the Scottish Highlands as if she were flying—Nell wasn't sure she cared.

'Alex.' Her voice didn't even sound like her own. Whose was it? Polly's?

No. Polly's voice held laughter and teasing and excitement.

This woman's voice was darker and warmer, a voice filled with passion and possibility.

She liked it.

It seemed as if Alex heard it too, because he let out a small groan as she said his name.

And then he was reaching down—or was she stretching up?—and they met in the middle, her lips burning as they touched his and she finally, finally tasted his kiss.

How could it feel like he'd waited millennia for a kiss he hadn't even realised he wanted until tonight? Okay, maybe a little longer—but not much.

He wanted Nell Andrews. And that might be the most surprising thing that might ever have happened to him in a lifetime of unexpected adventures.

More surprising than the date that stole his car, even.

Except...maybe it wasn't. Because he'd wanted her before, once, long ago. Maybe they were always heading back here.

They were unfinished business.

He pulled back just a little, to check Nell's eyes, her smile, to make sure she was there with him this time. From the soft smile and slightly glazed eyes that looked back at him, she was.

'You know, this is where you usually run out on me,' she murmured. 'Any moment now Fred is going to come calling, and you're going to rush off before your mates can see who you're kissing…'

His chest tightened. Looked like he wasn't the only one of them living in their past to-night. 'That's not… They needed me for something.' He couldn't say that wasn't what had happened, because it had. Yes, they'd needed his help, but that wasn't why he'd gone. They'd called and he'd run, spooked by the sudden shift in the world that had oc-curred when he'd kissed the most unlikely girl of all. He'd needed time to process, that was all. But then… 'You were gone when I came back.'

She shrugged. 'I realised what a ridiculous idea it was.'

And so she'd ignored him for the rest of the term, avoided every chance to be alone with him so they could talk.

Alex studied her carefully, took in that same defiance and defensiveness he'd seen at the top of the London Eye, and realised the truth. 'You mean you were scared.'

When she met his gaze with her own, she didn't try to hide the vulnerability behind it. 'Weren't you?'

He swallowed. 'Yes.'

How many years had it taken them to have this conversation? Too many.

There'd been something between them, something real, back then—and they'd both been too afraid to find out what it was. Maybe it was just chemistry, maybe it was really friendship—he wasn't sure either of them would accept anything more, even now. Still, he wondered if they could be any braver this time around.

'Are you scared now?' he asked.

'Terrified,' she admitted.

'Me too.' He tightened his arms around her waist. 'But I'm not going to run if you don't.'

Her lips curved into a smile as she reached up to kiss him again, and everything that had been tight and painful inside him seemed to relax at last.

Alex sank into their embrace, marvelling in the feel of Nell's sharp angles softening against him. He brought his hands up into the silky lengths of her hair, cradling the back of her head as he deepened the kiss, and wondered what luck or fate had brought them here again and given them a second chance at this.

Then the world jolted and Nell broke the kiss, and when Alex turned he saw the pilot trying—rather unsuccessfully—to hide his amusement.

'I did try to tell you we were landing,' he said. 'You were…preoccupied.'

Nell's head was buried against his chest. He had a suspicion she might be laughing.

Well. That or crying. He was hoping for the laughter.

'Nell! You made it!' At the sound of Polly's voice, Nell pulled away completely and Alex felt a chill in his chest at the loss.

Someone had brought over the steps for them to climb out of the basket, and Nell was gone before Alex could even speak to her. Even the pilot looked sympathetic as Alex hurried to follow. Was she running again? Really?

Nell glanced over her shoulder and caught his eye in the fading light, just before she reached her sister and her fiancé. And in that look Alex read everything she hadn't said.

No drama.

Right. Of course. Whatever this was, they weren't going to be making a big deal about it—especially not tonight, at Polly and Fred's engagement party. Probably not at any point between now and the wedding, if Alex knew Nell. And he hoped he was starting to.

If this was going to be anything at all, it

meant doing it according to Nell's rules. The last thing he wanted to do was spook her and remind her of all the reasons this was a crazy idea.

As long as she wasn't running from him this time, he could deal with everything else.

So he followed her over to meet the happy couple, and then onwards to his parents' house, and hoped that everyone could keep the drama in check tonight.

Because, that way, he might get to kiss Nell Andrews again. And honestly, right now, that was the only thing he could think about.

Nell hurried away from the hot-air balloon, her heart still pounding. She'd love to blame it on her fear of heights, but she knew it was caused by something else entirely.

Or someone.

All these years she'd been pretending to herself that he was the one who'd run away from their kiss, their closeness, back at university. But she knew that she was the one who'd run really. He'd tried to talk to her after, tried to regain that easy conversation they'd found that week—and she'd turned him away.

But she wasn't turning him away now, even if she probably should.

This is still as ridiculous as it was back then. We're still completely the wrong people for each other.

'Nell? You okay?' Polly wrapped an arm around her waist as they walked together towards the castle Alex called home. 'I'm sorry, I know heights aren't your thing, but I've *always* wanted a sunset hot-air balloon ride and—'

'It's fine,' she reassured her sister. 'If I really hadn't wanted to go, I'd have been even later than I was and just missed it. Besides, Alex kept me distracted.'

Polly looked between them suspiciously, but they both managed to keep their expressions innocent of exactly *how* Alex had been distracting her.

Nell sneaked a quick glance at Alex once Polly had looked away and caught the corner of his smile, the heat still smouldering in his eyes. She turned away.

Beside her, Polly was chattering on about the balloons, the guests, the late dinner they still had to eat. Nell listened with half an ear, but the rest of her brain had turned to something else.

Yes, she and Alex were incompatible in terms of a long-lasting, for ever love affair. That was undeniable.

But neither of them were looking for that, were they? They were looking for a date to the wedding. That was all.

Okay, maybe not all. Maybe she was looking for someone to remind her that she was desirable, or to show her a little fun after Paul's desertion. And maybe they both needed to exorcise some of the ghosts from their past. Find a little closure.

Maybe it didn't need to be anything more than that. Maybe she could have this—could have him—just for now, and without it needing to be a big drama. Or, actually, anyone else knowing about it at all.

Would that be so bad?

It's not the sort of thing Nell Andrews does, her brain reminded her.

But surely I'm *the only one who gets to decide that.*

Perhaps, just this once, and just for now, Nell Andrews could tiptoe along the wild side, without anyone else finding out.

And then she'd go back to looking for what she really wanted in life—stability, security, a predictable future.

Once she'd worked Alex McLeod out of her system.

'Ready for dinner?' Polly asked.

'More than ready,' Nell replied.

It had taken her years. But she was finally ready to give in to what she and Alex had discovered between them all those years ago at university.

Then she'd be able to move on.

CHAPTER TEN

ALEX HAD ALREADY resolved to give Nell some space before trying to talk to her about the kiss. He knew how she ran when she was cornered, and he wasn't going to make the mistake of spooking her again.

To that end, he threw himself back into the festivities for the time being. The hen and stag do featured a reduced and refined guest list—something that Alex was profoundly grateful for. Fred's cousin Jemima and her new boyfriend—Nell's ex, Paul—hadn't made the cut, so that was one less thing to disrupt things. Of his own ex-girlfriends, only three were friends with Polly in their own right. Teyla, who he'd dated in university and was now married to an investment banker, merely gave him the occasional disappointed look, as though he'd lived down to everything she'd always known he was capable of, so that was easy to deal with. Caitlin he avoided completely, which was definitely best for everyone, whatever Fred thought.

The third ex, Ursula, however, was a very different proposition. In fact, her propositions were exactly what he was trying to avoid, by the time they reached dessert.

'Do you remember the last time we were here together?' Ursula asked, while Alex silently cursed whoever had sat them together for dinner.

Both the stag and hen parties had been mixed together for the formal dinner in High Dudgeon House's main dining hall, sitting at long wooden tables that looked like they belonged in a historical movie. Much like many things in his childhood home, including the plumbing and the electrics.

It wasn't that they didn't have the money to fix those things. It was just that they were dull and boring, and his parents always had more interesting things to focus on.

That had never annoyed him before he'd got to know Nell again, these last few months.

Was boringness catching?

'Alex?' Beside him, Ursula nudged him with her pointy elbow. 'Do you remember?'

He blinked, and tried to cast his mind back. 'Last time we were here together was the night I introduced you to my parents.'

He'd thought he was introducing them to the woman he was going to marry. He'd planned to ask for his grandmother's ring the next day. There'd been a proposal plan all worked out, with a little help from Polly and Fred.

But it had also been the night his parents had invited their friends, the Hunters, to dinner—along with their son Patrick, who just happened to have gone to university with Ursula. One thing had led to another and…

'You didn't really think I was going to marry you, did you, Alex? Oh, you did. Oh, sweetie.'

His parents hadn't been surprised when Ursula had left that weekend with another man.

'The perils of passion,' his father had said.

'The highs and lows of love,' his mother had added.

For them, a little heartbreak was all part of the game—and that was how he'd come to see it too, since then. These days, he was more likely to be the one walking away without much of an apology. He played the game the same way everyone else did. High drama, high passion, a little adventure and a lot of fun—but nothing more.

And if he'd watched Fred and Polly sometimes and wondered how they managed to have both, he'd never admitted it to anyone. Until Nell, perhaps.

But the part he hadn't understood that weekend with Ursula, and wasn't sure he really understood now, was why. Why not him?

He glanced at her now, blonde and beautiful and smiling as if all of life was just a game. And beyond her he saw Nell, across on the other side of the table at the far end. Her hair fell like a black satin curtain, hiding half her face, but he could tell she wasn't having fun.

He wished he was sitting with her, rather than stuck here confronting his past.

But since he was...maybe it was time to ask the question that had been haunting him ever since.

'I remember you told me that weekend... you said, "You didn't really think I was going to marry *you*."'

'Did I?' Ursula at least had the grace to look ever so slightly embarrassed by that.

'I always wondered...why not? I thought we were happy together. Why were you so certain that we couldn't be happy for ever?'

'Because you didn't love me, Alex,' she replied bluntly. 'And I had a little more self-respect than to plan to marry a man who didn't love me.'

He blinked at her for a long moment. 'Of course I loved you.'

She shook her head and gave him a pitying smile. 'No, you didn't. Maybe you thought you did, because you grew up here, with your parents, and the only love you ever saw was based on grand gestures and blazing rows and performative reconciliations. And maybe that's what you were looking for. But it wasn't love, and it wasn't what I wanted.'

Alex rocked back in his chair as he absorbed the truth of what she was saying.

He *hadn't* loved Ursula, but he'd wanted to. He'd thought that the way they argued and made up was a sign of their mutual passion—of how much they cared.

Maybe it had really been a sign of their incompatibility.

Across on the other table he saw his parents glaring at each other as they bickered quietly. Soon, he knew, they'd stop being so quiet. After that, the whole room would know the details of their disagreement, and from there the old familiar pattern would continue.

The one they'd always told him was a sign of the depth of their love.

And for the first time Alex watched them and wondered if it was really a sign that they'd have been happier married to other people.

Then he saw the corner of his mother's smile as she took to her feet and denounced his father, and he knew they wouldn't be. They loved this, the drama, the passion, the way everyone was watching. This *was* love to them. The way he'd assumed it needed to be for him.

But maybe…maybe there was a different sort of love out there for him. Although as yet he had no idea what it might look like.

It definitely wasn't Nell's idea of love—never disagreeing about anything and never caring enough to even discuss it. He still wanted passion, and adventure.

Just…perhaps he could have that, without the high dudgeon and drama of his parents?

Something to think about, anyway.

'You genuinely look like I've rocked your world tonight,' Ursula said. 'Far more than I ever did when we were together. What on earth is going through your head?'

He looked away from his parents, and meant to turn his attention to the blonde at his side—but his gaze got caught on the silky curtain of Nell's hair, and the way her hunched shoulders told him she was hating every minute of this dinner.

Okay. That was enough waiting.

'I'm thinking I don't want to stay for the

after-dinner entertainment.' He pushed his chair back, stood up and went to grab Nell and finish what they'd started in that hot-air balloon.

Alex didn't seem to be having as much fun as he usually did at these things.

It wasn't as if Nell was in the habit of watching him at parties, but…okay, fine. Sometimes she watched him at parties.

He just always looked as if he was having so much fun. As if being around all those other people and talking too loud and getting talked into doing stupid things made him feel more alive.

It was a habit she'd got into at university, back when they were invited to a lot more parties anyway. Well, Polly and Fred were, and they'd drag Nell along, and Alex would just always be there because he knew *everybody.*

And he was always easy to pick out of a crowd, with his dark russet hair, tall frame and piercing blue eyes.

Of course she watched him. Most people did. He was very watchable.

And now, as she watched, she saw him push his chair back and stride towards her.

Her heart felt too loud in her chest—surely

everyone else could hear it too? Did they all know that she'd kissed Alex McLeod in a hot-air balloon?

No, because if Polly knew that she wouldn't have left Nell's side all evening, and would be demanding all the details right now. So nobody knew.

Except her and Alex. It was their own delicious secret. One she intended to keep close to her chest.

She lifted her head as he approached and met his gaze, warming as his mouth spread into a smile that seemed just for her. A smile full of promise.

A smile that told her he wasn't done with her yet.

She had no illusions about what this was between them. And she'd make sure he knew that too—that she wasn't expecting him to change, or for anything lasting to develop.

They were very different people.

But maybe, if they could just keep it between themselves—low-key, no drama—they might be able to explore all the passion that kiss had exposed between them.

'Get bored with your tablemates?' she asked as Alex dropped into the empty chair beside her. Nell didn't even know where her neighbour had disappeared to; she'd not paid him any attention throughout the meal, too busy watching Alex.

She just hoped he wasn't someone Polly had been trying to set her up with, or she might be in trouble with her twin later…

'Polly and Fred sat me next to my ex-girlfriend,' Alex replied. 'The one I thought I was going to marry until she ran off with the son of my parents' friends.'

Nell winced. 'Ah. Not ideal.'

'No. But maybe it wasn't the worst thing.'

A chill settled over her bare shoulders in her gown. Had she completely misread his expressions and his body language as he'd sat there? Had he really come over to tell her that their kiss had been a one-off and could never happen again, because he was getting back together with his ex?

It would be a suitably dramatic Alex thing to do. And yet she couldn't convince herself of it for longer than a second.

'How come?' She kept her voice level and reached for a spare bread roll someone hadn't eaten with their soup earlier.

'I'd never really had the chance to ask her what went wrong between us. Why she didn't want to marry me,' Alex explained.

Nell's eyebrows flew up without her permission. 'You *asked* her? *Tonight?*' Because only Alex could get into a deep dive on a past relationship, with the potential for an utter blowout, at someone else's engagement party. That was just drama waiting to happen.

He gave her a knowing smile. 'Relax. It was all very calm and amicable. No upstaging the bride and groom-to-be tonight, I promise.'

That, Nell decided, was a promise worth having.

'So did she tell you? I mean, you don't have to tell *me,*' she added hurriedly, realising that it might not be the kind of conversation a person wanted to share. 'But…do you feel better after the conversation?'

Alex tipped back in his chair, hands clasped behind his head, and looked contemplative. 'I don't know. I think so? She said… She told me I only thought that I was in love with her probably because my models of what love looks like weren't always top-notch. But that I never really did love her, not the way she deserved to be loved.'

'Was she right?' Nell asked softly.

He looked over at her, his eyes a little sad. 'Probably. I guess… I thought that all the arguing and the making-up, the passion, meant love. But now…' His gaze drifted away and, when she followed it, Nell realised he was looking at Polly and Fred. 'Maybe I have a better idea of what love should look like now.'

She knew how he felt. Polly and Fred, for all their dramas, were solid. There was a respect and a deep, deep love that transcended all of that.

Nell just wasn't sure that everyone was lucky enough to find that. And she wasn't willing to take a risk on something that might turn out to be just the drama, without the underpinnings.

Besides, she didn't want Alex thinking about marriage and for ever right now. She wanted him focusing on the idea of a wedding fling. With her.

'It's hard to imagine you getting married at all,' she said lightly. 'I mean, I wouldn't have thought it would be on your bucket list. Wouldn't a wife interfere with your life of wild adventures?'

'Maybe the right wife would come with me.' He flashed her a smile, but it faded quickly.

She wondered if he was realising the same thing she already had—that she'd never be that wife. She wasn't that person, and she didn't want to be.

Which meant that whatever had started between them in the hot-air balloon had a built-in expiry date.

Still, that didn't mean they couldn't enjoy it while it lasted. Did it?

'Earlier,' Alex said cautiously. 'In the hot-air balloon...'

'You kissed me,' Nell finished for him.

He gave her a look. 'An observer might say that you kissed me.'

'But a gentleman never would.'

That earned her a laugh. 'Nobody has ever called me a gentleman. Scottish castle notwithstanding.'

'True.' She shifted on her chair so she was facing him, her body curved towards his. 'So. We kissed. What about it?'

'Well, I wondered if that might be the sort of thing you'd enjoy doing again,' Alex said.

'The *sort* of thing?' She put on her best naive and quizzical look. 'Are you proposing a different sort of kissing? Or something else entirely?'

Alex leaned closer, his mouth almost beside her ear. 'Nell Andrews, I'm asking you if I can *finally* take you to bed tonight, and ravish you to within an inch of your life.' He sat back up. 'Now. Is *that* something you might be interested in?'

Every nerve-ending in her body was on

fire, as if her blood was burning them up as it pumped too fast around her body, fired up by her overacting heart.

She glanced towards the head of the table, where Fred and Polly sat, and noticed her sister watching them curiously. That would never do. The last thing she wanted was Polly getting wind of anything between her and Alex, and deciding that it was True Love and must be stage-managed by her so Nell couldn't screw it up.

If she wasn't careful, Polly would have planned them a double wedding by the time they made it to the Seychelles for the ceremony and celebrations.

Nell pulled her chair back, adding a little distance between her and Alex. Ever sensitive to her shifting moods, Alex did the same, with only a brief flash of disappointment on his face.

'That's a no, then?' he said without censure.

Nell flicked her gaze to her sister once more and, once she was sure Polly was distracted by a conversation with another guest, looked Alex dead in the eye.

'That's a hell, yes, please, if you can find a way we can do it without my sister ever knowing about it.'

The surprised smile that spread across Alex's handsome face didn't do anything to calm her racing heart.

'Oh, I'm sure I can come up with something,' he promised.

Nell thought she really liked his promises. Almost as much as his smiles.

CHAPTER ELEVEN

IT TOOK A little ingenuity—and a lot of patience—to avoid Polly's attention for the rest of the evening. But, just as Alex had predicted to himself, Nell's red line was drawn just before her sister. She didn't want Polly—or anyone else—knowing about things between them, and he had to respect that.

It wasn't as if he didn't understand why.

So, with a smile and a wink, he left Nell alone for the rest of the meal, waiting until the after-dinner mints and coffees were cleared, and the requisite speeches had been made. He rather thought Polly and Fred were testing him for what he might find to say in his wedding toast, so he got all the most embarrassing stories from university out of the way while the assembled company would appreciate them.

Nell, he noticed, was bright red and staring at the ceiling through most of them, as if she were embarrassed to even be associated with them. Which might be the case.

After dinner there was more drinking and dancing planned, with a DJ commandeering the ballroom of the house. His parents, he noticed, had been briefly distracted from their own drama by dessert, and then the cocktail bar Polly had arranged. If he was lucky, they'd forget about causing a scene until tomorrow.

As long as they didn't ruin his plans tonight, he didn't care.

Even with everything that was going on, the night seemed to drag. Alex tried to focus on the fun, but his mind was filled with the possibilities the night held *after* the party was over.

For the most part, he tried to keep his distance from Nell, worried that his thoughts would be written all over his face if anyone—namely Polly—saw them together. But, finally, he couldn't wait any longer.

He brushed past Nell as casually as he could, on his way through the ballroom, and took the opportunity to murmur instructions to her. 'Give it ten minutes, then tell Polly you're heading to bed.'

'You think she'll let me?' Nell asked.

Alex shrugged. 'You've already suffered

a hot-air balloon ride *and* my speech for her tonight. I think she'll take pity.'

'And what will you be doing?'

'Giving myself an alibi.' He smirked as he headed off towards the cocktail bar.

He kept half an eye on Nell across the ballroom, while chatting with a group of old university friends, so he knew the moment she approached Polly.

'Ten minutes on the dot,' he murmured to himself, earning a confused look from the woman he was talking to.

He waited until she'd left for bed, and Polly was dancing with Fred, to announce that it was time for shots.

'Just like back at uni!' he declared, as he procured some solid silver trays from one of the cabinets that lined the walls, and filled them with plastic shot glasses from behind the bar. A couple of bottles of tequila later, and he was handing them around to anyone still standing.

Even Polly and Fred joined in, looking amused at his throwback to their wilder university days.

'Same old Alex,' he heard more than one person say as he passed by with his trays.

He tried to ignore the way the words stung. Hadn't he grown up at all?

Perhaps not. Nell obviously didn't think so.

Nell. That was who this was all about. He had to focus on the endgame, here.

Three trays of shots later, he decided that everyone in the room would vouch that he'd been there all night, causing mayhem. He wondered if he needed something more dramatic to cement the idea that he'd partied to the death in people's minds, but he was too impatient to come up with anything.

After all, Nell was waiting for him.

He knew the castle better than any of the guests so it was easy enough for him to slip out unseen, through one of the doors only the servants really used, since it led directly into the kitchens. From there, he made his way up the back staircase to the first floor, where the wedding party had all been given rooms. He almost wished Nell had been housed out in one of the converted barns or old labourers' cottages with the other guests instead. It would have given them more privacy for everything he had planned…

Oh, well. The stone walls were thick at High Dudgeon House. Probably no one would hear anything anyway.

Because he was determined to make Nell Andrews scream his name tonight.

He crept along the first-floor landing, shoes

silent on the runner carpet. He'd done this often enough in his youth to know exactly where the creaking floorboards were. Not that he thought anyone would hear them over the noise of the party downstairs, but at some point it had just become habit.

Nell's room was fortuitously next to his own childhood room, where he still slept whenever he visited. In fact, the room she'd been assigned had once been his nanny's bedroom—which cast up a number of disturbing connotations, but also meant there was a very convenient connecting door between the two.

Alex slipped into his own room, crossed it swiftly and knocked on the connecting door.

Another woman might have answered it in lingerie, or at least some sort of slinky nightgown. Another woman might have just called for him to come in, where he would have found her naked in the bed.

Nell yanked the door open, still wearing her ballgown and a serious frown, and said, 'What did you do?'

He blinked uncomprehendingly at her. 'What do you mean?'

'You said you were giving yourself an alibi. So, what kind of scene did you cause? Does my sister hate you for ever? If you ruined their engagement party just so you could sleep with me—'

Alex stepped forward, put his hands on her bare shoulders and smiled down at her. 'While I would do many things to sleep with you tonight, darling, I know better than to think you'd still want to sleep with *me* if I ruined anything about this wedding for Polly and Fred.'

Some of the tension flowed out of her shoulders, and he felt them relax under his fingers. She really was far too tense. The woman needed a good massage. Or several incredible orgasms.

Maybe he could help with both those things.

'So what *did* you do?' she asked again, more curious than accusing this time.

'I served trays of tequila shots to basically everybody in that room,' he replied. 'Everyone saw me partying hard. Nobody is likely to notice that I've disappeared early—and, if they do, they'll just think I'm sleeping off the tequila somewhere.'

'Oh.' Nell's mouth curved up into a smile. 'That doesn't sound too bad.'

'Does that mean I can come in?' He stepped a little closer, until his body was flush against hers, and was rewarded by the way her cleavage swelled over the neckline of her gown when she breathed in sharply.

God, this woman did things to him. It was quite a relief to see that he did the same to her.

Nell stepped away. 'Come in, Alex.'

He took a breath, glad he'd only had one of those tequila shots.

He wanted to remember every moment of this night.

Just in case he never got another one with her.

Nell stared at Alex across the room, and wondered at the incredibly weird sequence of events that had brought them here.

They were going to have sex.

In a Scottish castle.

At her sister's engagement party.

And this was the strangest one...

Together.

She was going to sleep with Alex McLeod. Finally.

And however outlandish and unpredictable that idea was...suddenly she couldn't wait a moment more.

Reaching up behind her, she tugged down the zip of her ballgown and let it fall.

It was over-the-top, slightly awkward and maybe a little dramatic—and it made Alex's eyes widen to saucer-size. So that made it worth it.

'You still wear the best lingerie,' he said, his voice husky, and Nell felt the heat hit her cheeks as she looked down at herself.

The strapless corset had been almost a necessity under the off-the-shoulder ballgown. The fact it was zebra-print…well, it was still black and white, wasn't it? Just like all her other clothes.

And the matching thong just made sense.

Alex stared at her a moment longer, until she started to worry he might have changed his mind.

Then he lunged forward, crossing the room in the time it took her to blink, and suddenly she was in his arms and…

Everything else faded away.

The drama of the moment, the fear and the tension, the worry of all the ways things could go wrong, the lingering doubt about whether any of this was a good idea in the first place—even the nagging feeling that Polly was going to knock on her door at any moment and catch them.

The moment Alex's lips touched hers she forgot it all.

'God, I've been waiting to do that again all night,' he murmured as he rested his forehead against hers and smiled down at her. ‘You looked beautiful in that ballgown, in case I hadn’t mentioned it.’

‘You hadn’t, actually.’

His lips twitched as if he were holding in his laughter. ‘Well, you look even more amazing in this.’

Alex ran his hands up the side of her corset, over the boning that kept everything in place, and Nell shivered.

‘Want to see what I look like out of it?’

Alex groaned. ‘God, yes, please.’

‘Then take it off.’

Where had the courage come from to make her say that? To do any of this?

Nell had no idea.

But she wasn’t going to argue with it.

Maybe tonight—just this one night—she could give in to the passion, adventure and drama that was her genetic birthright and have wild, unashamed, uninhibited sex with Alex McLeod.

Tomorrow, she’d go back to being cautious, careful Nell. She’d resume her search for stability and surety in her life.

But tonight… Tonight she felt like someone else entirely.

Alex’s nimble fingers made short work of loosening the corset laces at her back, looking down over her shoulder as he worked, his chest pressed against hers. She wondered if he could feel her racing heartbeat between them. If his blood was pounding in his ears the way hers was.

Then he stepped back and the corset fell to the floor, leaving her bare except for her zebra-print thong, the thigh-high stockings she'd worn under her dress and the heeled lace-up boots she'd chosen instead of high heels. She swallowed as she realised Alex was still fully dressed, his bow tie hanging loose around his neck, but his jacket still on.

She should feel vulnerable. Embarrassed.

Instead, she felt powerful.

His gaze raked over every inch of her, drinking her in. She gave him a moment to adjust, then stretched out her hand.

'Take me to bed, Alex.'

He met her gaze and she saw his throat bob as he swallowed. 'With pleasure.'

Making love to Nell Andrews was like nothing he'd ever imagined. Not that he'd spent a lot of time imagining it over the years since she'd run out on him—or he'd run out on her. But if he had...he'd have thought she'd have been buttoned-up. A lights off, missionary kind of girl, not that there was anything wrong with that.

He'd have thought she'd find the whole thing embarrassing.

The kisses they'd shared before had been too tentative, too uncertain, to give much away. But tonight…tonight he'd known the moment he'd kissed her in the hot-air balloon that things were different this time. He'd felt the passion surging through her, and known that the two of them together could be something very special indeed.

He just hadn't expected *this*.

He wasn't some fumbling teenage boy. He knew what to do to make a woman's toes curl, how to get her to pant his name desperately in his ear. How to take control in the bedroom and ensure that everyone had a fantastic time.

Except…

From the moment she dropped her ballgown and revealed the lingerie she was wearing underneath, Alex didn't feel in control at all.

In fact, he'd never felt so out of control.

'You're wearing too many clothes,' she murmured, reaching for the buttons on his shirt.

How could he have never realised there was this side to her before? They'd known each other for a decade. All that time, this woman—filled with passion and possibility—had been hiding behind the boring rules she imposed on her own life.

He should have known. He should have realised the first time he'd seen her lingerie drawer. The first time he'd kissed her, when they were idiot teens.

But he knew now, and he wasn't going to waste another second.

Together, they stripped off his shirt and jacket in one go, and as she sat on the edge of the bed and moved on to dealing with his trousers he eased off her boots, then her thong, leaving the stockings in place. Then he stepped out of his boxers, and looked down at the glory of her.

'What?' she asked, stretching for him on the bed.

What little blood there had been left in his brain fled to where all the rest had gone, and he knew he'd never been this hard, this desperate for a woman before.

'I'm just trying to decide where to start,' he said. 'I want to kiss every inch of you before sunrise. Twice.'

She smiled. 'Better get a move on, then.'

So he did.

He kissed down her throat to her breasts,

spending precious moments on each—then lingering longer when he heard the sweet gasping noises she made when he did. Finally, he moved lower, skipping down her thighs to kiss up her calves through her stockings, teasing the place where the silk gave way to even smoother skin.

'Alex, for the love of all things holy…'

'Patience,' he told her.

He'd taken so long to really see her, he wasn't going to rush now.

But eventually he couldn't wait any longer. He shifted closer, spreading her legs as he moved his mouth nearer to where he knew she wanted it. She tensed, just for a moment, though, which gave him pause.

'Okay?' he asked softly.

She nodded. 'I will be. When you get to the good stuff.'

Smirking, he got to the good stuff.

And God, was it good. The way she writhed under his tongue. The sounds she made as he worked her all the way to the brink…then stopped.

'I always knew you were a bad man,' she said, her voice hoarse.

He kissed his way over her belly and between her breasts as he slid up her body. 'I want to feel you come around me.'

She wriggled against him in a way that made him clench his jaw and desperately hold onto his self-control. 'I can live with that, I suppose.'

She might be able to, but Alex was kind of afraid the experience might kill him.

At the least, he already knew that moving on from this night was going to be difficult.

Maybe even impossible.

CHAPTER TWELVE

NELL GRABBED HOLD of Alex's arms as he slid inside her, and experienced the same strange weightlessness she'd felt on the hot-air balloon. As if the whole world had fallen away and she was floating out of space and time.

Then everything came back into focus and she moved with him, catching his rhythm, desperately chasing that high his tongue and fingers had promised her.

'God, Nell.' His voice was hot and harsh in her ear. 'We should have been doing this for years.'

She was beyond the words she needed to respond, but she suspected the noises she did make were enough to tell him she agreed. He chuckled in response, and tilted his hips just so and—

Nell had always thought books were exaggerating when they talked about heroines seeing fireworks behind their eyes when they came.

Apparently it had just been another one of

those things that was outside her sphere of experience.

Maybe some things were worth taking risks for.

'You still with me?' Alex asked, starting to sound ragged himself.

'Just about.'

'Want to see if we can get you there again?'

It was on the tip of her tongue to tell him not to bother. That she'd never orgasmed twice in one night, with anyone. That he should just let go and finish this.

Except…

This was her night for taking risks. And maybe she wanted to see if she could.

She nodded, and he started to move again, hot and heavy and wonderful inside her and over her, moving one hand down to the place they were joined, and it didn't take very long at all for her to realise that, yes, actually, this was something else she was very, very capable of. If she just let herself go…

This time, he fell over the edge with her, collapsing half on her, half to the side, after choking out her name. Nell lay beside him, slowly getting her breath back, hot and sweaty and satisfied.

'You're smiling,' Alex said, before sitting

up to dispose of the condom. 'Guess I must have done something right at last.'

'Not you,' Nell told him. 'Us. We're good at that.'

He lay back beside her and wrapped an arm tight around her waist. 'We really, really are.'

They lay in contented silence for a while, long enough that she began to suspect he'd fallen asleep. She wanted to do the same, her whole body begging for rest, but she needed to get out of these stockings. And she couldn't sleep until she'd cleaned her teeth, not to mention taken off her make-up. Plus she should really send him back to his own room, in case Polly came looking for her first thing, and—

'Do you always think so loud after sex?' Alex asked, the words slightly slurred with sleep.

'I think this loud all the time,' she admitted. 'You're just not usually close enough to hear it.'

Which was, she knew, a ridiculous thing to say, given that nobody could hear another person *think*. But from the way his lips curved against the skin of her shoulder, before he placed a light kiss there, he seemed to appreciate the comment all the same.

Alex sighed and then, with what appeared to be considerable effort, sat up beside her.

'Go on,' he said. 'I know you want to go clean up or whatever. So, go do that. And then we'll talk about whatever has your mind whirring like a clock.'

She didn't argue. Which might have been a first for them, actually.

It was only once she was locked safely in the en suite bathroom that the enormity of what she'd just done crashed down on her.

She'd slept with Alex McLeod. And it had been *incredible.*

To her surprise, she found she didn't regret any of what had happened at all. Her mind was just hung up on what came next.

Which she supposed was what she needed to talk to Alex about.

She took a moment to smile at her reflection in the mirror—a flushed, relaxed Nell she almost didn't recognise smiled back.

Then she set about cleaning up, and getting back to Alex.

The sooner they talked, the sooner she could sleep.

Alex ducked back into his own room while Nell was in the bathroom, leaving the connecting door open so she wouldn't think he'd run out on her if she came out before he returned. He washed quickly in his own bathroom, and pulled on a pair of comfortable joggers—High Dudgeon House got cold at night, he knew from his childhood.

He was glad he had, though, when he heard a knock on his own bedroom door.

Fred stood on the other side, his eyes a little glassy—probably due to the tequila, Alex assumed. Hopefully the drinks had had enough of an impact that he wouldn't notice the open connecting door.

'There you are!' Fred clapped him on the shoulder with a wide smile. 'We were wondering where you'd got to! Polly thought you might have sloped off with some woman, but I was blaming the tequila—remember that night in Mexico? You and tequila never were good friends.'

Alex forced a laugh. 'Yeah, tequila might not have been my best ever plan. You and Polly had fun though?'

'Of course! Great party.' Fred looked both ways along the landing, then lowered his voice. 'Although you, ah, might want to check on your parents in the morning. Last I saw, your mother was deep in conversation with old Calvin Brooks.'

Alex winced. Calvin had to be fifteen years his mother's junior, and a friend of a friend of a friend who had somehow ended up on the invite list for the weekend despite Polly's best efforts. 'Right. I'll deal with that tomorrow. Right now I just want to—' He jerked a thumb towards the bathroom, remembering too late about the open door.

Luckily, Fred didn't seem to notice it. 'Yeah, sure. And I'd better find my room. Polly's waiting, you know?' He waggled his eyebrows and wandered off.

Alex shut the door and rested his head against the wood for a moment, then turned to see that the connecting door had been pushed almost completely closed.

Only almost, though. That meant he was still welcome, right?

He knocked anyway, and found Nell waiting right behind the door.

'Fred came looking for you?' She looked up at him, chewing on her lower lip.

The stockings were gone, he realised. In their place were tartan pyjama bottoms, and a loose T-shirt that still left him thinking about everything he now knew was under it.

'Yeah. He thinks the tequila got to me and I had to go lie down. Or throw up. Or something.' So much for his reputation as a partier. Ah, well. It had been worth it.

More than worth it.

Nell sat on the edge of her bed, and for the

first time Alex took a proper look around the room. 'You know, this used to be my nanny's room.'

She gave a surprised laugh, then covered her face. 'I was about to say that I don't know if that makes things better or worse. But I do know. It's worse. Much worse.'

Alex moved to sit beside her, leaving just enough space between them that he hoped she wouldn't feel crowded. 'If it helps, I never thought about my nanny the way I think about you.'

Nell peeked out from between her fingers. 'And how *do* you think about me?'

'I didn't make that clear enough earlier? Because I can show you again…well, if you give me a little recovery time first…'

'That's not what I mean.' Dropping her hands to her lap, she took a deep breath, and Alex knew that she'd probably been planning whatever she said next in the mirror before she came out. Which meant that it was important, and he should pay proper attention.

It was just hard to do that when her breasts kept shifting under that T-shirt…

'I had a great time with you tonight,' she said. 'Better than I could have expected. I wouldn't have thought…knowing you and knowing myself, that we could be so compatible. But, well, we were, I think.' She looked to him for confirmation, and he nodded emphatically.

'Hell, yes, definitely compatible,' he said. 'But I know what you mean. I wouldn't have naturally assumed you and I would be either.'

'So I guess what I'm asking is…what happens next?' She looked up at him, eyes wide and her mouth looking strangely vulnerable, still pink and swollen from his kisses. Thank God Fred hadn't seen her, or he'd have known instantly what they'd been up to. 'I mean, we might be compatible here, in the bedroom. But outside it…'

The reality of what she was saying hit hard into his post-coital afterglow. 'We're not.'

It wasn't a new thought. He'd had one very similar just a few hours earlier, when talking to Ursula.

However much he wanted Nell physically, emotionally and personally they wanted completely different things. He was never going to be able to offer her the safe, secure, boring life she wanted. And she had no desire to join him in a life of adventure.

But maybe that was okay. Maybe they didn't need to.

'Well, perhaps we just…lean into our strengths and ignore the rest?' he suggested.

'So we just keep having sex indefinitely and otherwise ignore each other completely?' She sounded, not unreasonably, a little sceptical about the plan. But really, what else did they have?

'Unless you want to cause a scene and dump me dramatically at your sister's wedding?'

She rolled her eyes. 'Does that sound like something I would do?'

'No,' he admitted. 'But neither does sleeping with me in the first place.'

'True.'

He nudged her with his shoulder and she leaned into him, a welcome warmth against his side.

'The way I see it, we have three options.' He raised one finger. 'One, pretend this never happened, and go back to being mere business partners and occasionally friendly acquaintances.'

'Hmm. Seems unlikely,' Nell said. 'For starters, sex like that is pretty hard to forget.'

'Agreed. Which brings us to option two.' He held up two fingers. 'Fall madly in love and try to change each other so we can live in harmony together for ever.'

'With our pet unicorn, I take it?'

'Obviously.'

She gave him a look.

'Taking that as a no, it leaves us with number three.' He added the third finger. 'Try being friends. Perhaps with occasional short-term intimate advantages. At least until after the wedding.'

'More best man with benefits than friends with benefits?' Nell tilted her head as if she was actually considering it, which was, if he was honest, more than Alex had actually hoped for.

'If you like.'

'I suppose it *could* work,' she said thoughtfully. 'Although there'd have to be some ground rules.'

'I never expected anything less.' Nell was the *queen* of rules and boundaries, after all. She was the reason they had the laminated poster with coffee machine etiquette in the kitchen at work.

'Polly and Fred never know.' She gave him an intense, defiant look. 'That's a dealbreaker. Because if Polly found out…'

She trailed off, leaving Alex wondering exactly what Polly would do if she *did* find out. Disapprove? Try to marry them off? Something in between?

Whatever it was, it was enough to worry Nell, so he agreed. 'Okay. What else?'

Nell bit down on her lip as she looked up at

him. 'It's only until after the wedding. Okay? I just… I don't want to risk either of us getting too comfortable in an arrangement that can't last.'

'That makes sense,' he replied, even as a sinking part of his heart realised that the wedding was only a few weeks away. Why had they wasted the last couple of months dating other people? 'We can get it all out of our system between now and then.'

'Exactly,' Nell said firmly. 'Then we can both get back to trying to find real dates we might have a future with.'

'Great,' Alex said.

Even though the idea of Nell with another boring date who didn't understand her turned his stomach.

Maybe he could just blame the tequila.

CHAPTER THIRTEEN

POLLY SWEPT INTO the meeting room on Monday morning looking for all the world like she'd spent the weekend relaxing at a spa, rather than drinking and partying on her hen do, as Nell knew she actually had. The sheer quantity of empty bottles at the end of the weekend had surprised even Mr and Mrs McLeod.

Separately, of course, since they weren't speaking by that point, and Mrs McLeod had her cases packed by the front door with everyone else's as they were leaving.

According to Alex, that was par for the course. Nell had no idea how he lived with it.

'Well, I think that went well, don't you?' Polly said, glancing around the table with a fond look for her fiancé, and satisfied ones for Alex and Nell. Until she frowned. 'Except neither of you has a date for my wedding yet, do you?'

Nell pointedly did not look at Alex as she shook her head.

'I had high hopes for you, McLeod, after you disappeared on Saturday night,' Polly went on. 'But Fred tells me you were in your room alone, recovering from the tequila shots you insisted on. Which probably serves you right, but doesn't get you any closer to a date for the wedding.'

'Sorry to be such a disappointment,' Alex said drily, and just the sound of his voice made Nell clench her thighs together to avoid shivering.

When she risked a glance up she saw that Fred was giving her a funny look, so she reached for her notebook and started leafing through the pages, as if she might find a date inside.

No need to tell the bride and groom that she already had one. They wouldn't understand, anyway.

It had been a relief to realise that she and Alex were on the same page there. They were too different for anything between them to grow beyond the inevitable heartbreak that would ensue when they both accepted that.

Giving themselves the deadline of the wedding removed that risk. And made the next few weeks all the more intense...

At the head of the table, Polly sat down with a dramatic sigh. 'Well, that's it then. You're just going to have to pair up for the wedding. I know you don't want to,' she said, holding up a hand to forestall the expected objections. 'But I can't have the maid of honour and best man going solo at a romantic, couple themed wedding!'

'Everything *is* planned for twos,' Fred added solemnly. Nell suspected he found this whole thing as ridiculous as she did, but had decided to go along with it for the sake of peace and harmony.

Of course, she also suspected that Polly had only planned it this way in the first place to showcase the agency's best work, but now it seemed to have taken on a life of its own.

With a sigh, she cast a careful look in Alex's direction. 'What do you think?'

Leaning back in his chair, Alex shrugged, his expression bland and emotionless. 'Doesn't make much difference to me at this point. *You* were the one who refused to partner me to the wedding in the first place. *Not a chance in hell,* were your exact words, as I recall.'

Nell bit the inside of her cheek to keep from laughing. She really had said that, hadn't she? 'I don't think I was exactly your first choice either,' she pointed out.

'Well, apparently you're my last.' He sighed. 'What do you say, Andrews? Think you can face putting up with me for the wedding week?'

'We don't have to share a room or anything, do we?' she asked Polly in mock panic.

Polly laughed. 'Even I'm not that cruel. But I will have to put you together in one of the two-bedroom beachfront villas—it would just be a waste, otherwise.'

'Fair enough, I suppose.' Nell tried not to sound too enthusiastic about the idea, but inside she was cheering. They wouldn't even have to sneak around between rooms if they were sharing a villa!

Polly went on, 'And Alex, I'd appreciate it if you could manage not to split up any of the other couples over the wedding week.' When he pulled a wide-eyed, innocent look, she added, 'I saw how chummy you and Ursula were getting again over dessert. But she's coming with Damien, and I have high hopes for the pair of them, so don't go ruining it.'

'My little matchmaker,' Fred said fondly.

'I just want everyone to be as happy as we are.' Polly took his hand across the table and gave him a frankly sickening smile.

Nell exchanged a quick glance with Alex. 'As long as you're not making any plans for us two. This is strictly a wedding-only arrangement.'

'Over the moment you two jet off on your honeymoon,' Alex agreed.

'Yes, yes, I know.' Polly flapped a hand in acknowledgment. 'Frankly, I've given up on the two of you. Alex will never risk settling down long enough to find love, probably because he doesn't want to end up like his parents, which, having witnessed them this weekend, I suppose is fair enough. And Nell, you'll never risk your safe and boring life to fall properly, deeply, irrevocably in love, even if you leave your flat or your office long enough to find someone!' She took a deep breath and looked around at the others, who sat in stunned silence. 'What?'

Fred squeezed her hand. 'Maybe a couple too many home truths for a Monday morning, sweetheart.'

Polly looked mulishly unrepentant. 'Well, if I don't tell them, who will? They're never going to be happy at this rate.'

Alex got to his feet. 'And on that note, I think I'm going to take my unlovable self off to get a coffee. Coming, Andrews?'

'Why not? After all, I'll never find love if I hide out in my office, will I?'

'I think the guy at the coffee cart was flirting with you last week,' Alex said.

Nell clasped her hands together in pretend joy. 'Well, thank goodness! My spell in the love wilderness is over at last.'

'You two are being ridiculous,' Polly said sulkily. 'I just meant—'

'Oh, we know what you meant,' Alex broke in. 'And I'm sure we each thank you for the early morning psychoanalysis.'

'But I've got an octogenarian coffee guy to flirt with,' Nell added. 'Bye!'

Leaving the meeting room door to swing shut behind them, Alex and Nell headed down the stairs and out into the bright, early summer London morning.

'Well, I think that went well, don't you?' Alex said as they reached the edge of the park, and what Nell had come to think of as *their* coffee cart came into sight.

'I don't think they suspected anything, if that's what you mean,' Nell replied. 'But I'm slightly concerned that this bridezilla thing might lead to my sister wanting to take control of *everyone's* lives.'

'You say that like she didn't already,' Alex pointed out.

'True.' Nell nudged his arm with her shoulder. 'But this, us…for the next two weeks, at least. That's none of her business.'

'Agreed.' Alex pressed a kiss to the top of her hair. 'It's just us. So, coffee?'

'God, yes, please.'

Neither of them mentioned what Polly had said about each of them. Which, Nell decided later that night, lying in her bed with Alex, was probably for the best.

Why ruin something good with reality before they had to?

Alex awoke two weeks later, warm and content and with thoughts of waking Nell up to see if her train of thought was running the same way his was…when he realised the other half of the bed was empty.

He frowned. He was pretty sure she'd been there when he went to sleep. And, not that he liked to brag, by the time they'd called it a night her legs definitely hadn't been capable of carrying her home.

Who was he kidding? He *loved* to brag about that.

Not that he did or could. Because nobody else could know about them. Their entire relationship was invisible to the outside world.

And now Nell herself had disappeared.

'Andrews?' he called out, into the empty

room. They'd gone back to his flat the night before, after eating dinner at some tiny restaurant in a part of London he didn't think he'd ever visited before, and knew Polly and Fred wouldn't. Even so, Nell hadn't allowed him to so much as hold her hand, just in case.

That way, if anyone sees us, we can tell them it was a last minute wedding planning meeting, or something, she'd said.

If he didn't know better, he'd think she was ashamed of him.

But he did know better. Which was why he was pretty sure she was ashamed of herself—for wanting him in the first place. For desiring something so far out of her comfort zone as sex with him.

Just sex. Nothing more. That much had been made very clear.

And it *was* for the best. He knew that.

He just...didn't like to think too much about what happened when the wedding was over.

The wedding.

Wait.

Alex sat up suddenly. 'Nell?'

She appeared in the doorway this time, fully dressed in some stretchy black trousers, a stripy black and white T-shirt and a long black cardigan. She was putting a golden hoop earring through her lobe.

'Why are you still in bed? I woke you up before I went for my shower!'

'You did?' Now that he thought about it, maybe he vaguely recalled her murmuring something into his ear, a while ago.

'Yes!' She rolled her eyes. 'Get up. Get dressed. The cab to the airport will be here in thirty minutes!'

Airport. Yes.

Because the wedding week started today, with their flight to Mahé departing that afternoon.

'Bet you're glad I made you pack last night now,' Nell shot back over her shoulder, before she disappeared into the living room.

Alex hauled himself out of bed, showered and dressed in something comfortable for flying, then joined her.

'What are you doing?' he asked.

'Checking our passports and tickets,' Nell replied, not looking up from the special travel folder she'd placed them in.

'You did that last night,' he pointed out.

'And at least four times already this morning.' She looked faintly apologetic as she said it.

'So we've definitely got them, then?'

'Looks like.' She hugged the wallet to her chest. 'Do you think anyone will notice if

I've got your travel documents though? Will they guess?'

He shrugged. 'Probably people will be more worried about their own stuff. And if they notice…well, you're in charge of making sure I don't screw up this week, right?' He was sure Polly must have added that to the list of maid of honour duties once he and Nell were paired up for the wedding.

'That's true. And if I hadn't been here this morning you'd have probably slept through the cab coming, so…yeah, we can probably sell it.'

'Great. That's one less thing for me to worry about, then.'

Which didn't explain why a new weight of worry seemed to have landed in his chest over the last few days.

Was it just the fact that she was hiding everything that was between them from the world? He wasn't built for hiding away—he lived unapologetically out loud, and had never been good at pretending he felt something he didn't, or pretending he didn't feel what he did.

But she could never be happy opening up their feelings to the world that way. And what was the point arguing about it when they already had a built-in expiry date?

Oh.

Maybe *that* was the problem.

They were down to their last week together and…he didn't want it to end. Not yet. Not when they were having so much fun together—secrecy and her desire to organise him to within an inch of his life notwithstanding.

But they'd made a deal, and he wasn't going to go back on that now.

All he could do was make the most of the time they had left, then end things amicably—even happily. Then she'd be free to find someone who could give her what she needed and he…

Well. Maybe he'd get to keep her as a friend, after this.

That had to be better than nothing, right?

'You've got the rings?' Nell asked, and he nodded. 'And your suit?'

'You checked my case twice when I was packing it.'

'And you haven't changed anything since?' she pressed.

'No,' he said. 'You realise that airport security will be a breeze after this?'

The fact Nell didn't even make a joke about his previous dates and airport security told him how stressed she was. 'And I've got my dress, my shoes—you packed shoes, right?—and my jewellery…cufflinks! Did you pack cufflinks?'

'Yes. Because they were on the frighteningly comprehensive packing list you gave me.' He had never been so well organised for a trip in his life.

'Come on, then.' Nell grabbed the handle of her suitcase, their travel folder tucked under her arm. 'Let's get down there and wait for the cab.'

He followed docilely, and it was only once they were in the taxi on the way to the airport that he realised she'd booked it for six hours before their flight.

CHAPTER FOURTEEN

POLLY HAD CHARTERED a private plane to get the bulk of her guests to the island in the Seychelles, where she and Fred would be tying the knot. Ostensibly, this was just another example of what Here & Now could offer their clients, and as such was being dutifully uploaded to all their social media channels. In reality, Nell suspected her sister just wanted to keep all her guests in one place, where they couldn't get into trouble.

There were some guests travelling in from other countries, or arriving later in the week for some reason or another, but it was still a full plane heading out. Nell scanned the occupied seats as she boarded, relieved to see that the two guests she least wanted to spend time in an enclosed place with—her mother and Paul—didn't seem to be flying with them.

'I have never seen a plane quite this...pink,' Alex murmured over her shoulder. 'It's like Valentine's Day threw up in here.'

'I'm not entirely sure on the logistics of that, but I take your point.' Each pair of seats had a double-sized pink blanket for sharing, plus a tiny bag of heart-shaped chocolates wrapped in red foil. The overhead cabins had been decorated with pink hearts, and even the stewards were wearing red waistcoats with pink heart pockets.

'Want the window seat?' Alex asked, and she shook her head.

'The less I can see of the open, empty space below us the better.'

They settled into their seats, Alex sweeping the fluffy pink blanket across both their laps. Nell picked up the card placed in the pocket of the seat in front and surveyed the details of their flight.

'So, we have a choice of several romantic movies to watch, and all our food will apparently be heart-shaped.' She tossed the card to him, and he chuckled as he read it.

'Heart-shaped pancakes I can buy,' he said. 'But heart-shaped chicken?'

She snickered at the face he pulled, then glanced around self-consciously to see who was watching. Yes, they were supposed to be attending this wedding together, but not *together* together, and she didn't want anyone getting any ideas. Or guessing what was actually going on between them.

Which meant they probably shouldn't seem to be getting on *too* well. Or would that make things worse? Like they were protesting too much?

Nell wrestled with the uncertainty all through take-off, which served as a pleasant distraction. And at least she didn't feel too self-conscious about gripping tight to Alex's hand under their blanket.

As soon as the seatbelt sign had turned off, and they were cruising along at Nell didn't want to know what height, Polly popped up beside their seats. 'Isn't this wonderful?'

'It's a pastel pink wonderland,' Alex replied from by the window. 'I'm sure all of your fellow couples are loving it.'

Polly rolled her eyes. 'Okay, maybe it's a little over the top, but I wanted *romantic*.'

'It most certainly is that,' Nell said. If, by romantic, one meant pink and over the top.

Personally she preferred more private, intimate romantic gestures. But each to their own.

'I know it's a little weird for you two,' Polly went on. 'Not being an actual couple. But if you could just *pretend,* just for this week, just for me, that would be wonderful.'

Nell cast a quick glance back at Alex, who gave her a slightly lopsided smile and a shrug, as if to say it was all up to her.

But under the blanket she felt his hand resting on her thigh, his fingers inching up along the seam of her leggings.

'I'm sure we can manage that,' she replied, her mouth suddenly painfully dry.

Polly beamed. 'Thank you!' Then she bounced off towards the next set of guests.

And Alex's fingers inched higher.

Alex watched the back of Polly's head as she moved further down the plane, away from them. Then he teased the inside of Nell's thigh just a little more.

Any moment now he expected her to grab his hand and move it, to glare at him and whisper for him to stop playing games.

But she didn't.

So he ran his knuckles up the inside of her other thigh too, and smiled when he heard her suck in a sharp breath.

'Alex,' she whispered. 'Someone might see.'

He gazed around them pointedly. Every other passenger was engrossed in their own occupation—a movie, a book, conversation with their own partner. More than a few had their blankets spread across them, some napping, some…well, Alex wasn't going to judge what might be going on under them. Especially right now.

He inched his fingers closer to her centre.

'Nobody is looking. Nobody cares. Nobody is thinking about what you and I are up to here.' Or anywhere, for that matter.

Nell seemed to think the sky would fall down if people found out about them, but he wasn't so sure. Would anyone really care as much as she thought?

'We're on a plane,' Nell hissed. 'In public.'

But even as she said the words she tilted her hips just so, giving his wandering fingers better access.

He smiled. 'Do you want me to stop, then?'

He would, if she said the words. Of course he would.

But she didn't.

'No,' she breathed, her cheeks pink. 'Don't stop.'

'Okay, then.'

Alex twisted his body, wishing she'd chosen the window seat. It would make doing this undetected so much easier. Still, he'd been right when he said that nobody was paying them any attention.

'Think you can be quiet?' he murmured as his fingertips reached the top of the seam.

Nell nodded, her bottom lip caught between her teeth.

'Good.' He pressed down, just a little harder, and heard her breath kick up a notch. Perfect.

The angles weren't ideal and with the blanket over them he could only rely on touch to figure out what she needed. He wished he could pull down her leggings and get inside, but he had a feeling she'd draw the line before then and push him away.

So he'd work with what he had. Better to touch her this way than not at all.

Better to be a secret than to not have her...

He pushed the thought away. This wasn't their relationship he was focusing on, purely her pleasure. A chance for her to do something adventurous, unexpected and fun.

He'd bet none of her exes had ever made her orgasm on a plane before.

With a renewed sense of purpose, he traced a finger along the seam of her leggings again, and watched her bite down harder on her lip. He smiled, and prepared to take her higher—

'Hi, guys.' Fred leaned against Nell's seat, looming over them. 'Nell, can we swap seats for a bit? Polly wants to run through some wedding bits with you before we land. Okay?'

'Absolutely.' Nell's cheeks were burning

red as she slipped out from under the blanket, moving away from her seat without even looking back at Alex.

With a sigh, Alex slumped into his own seat, pulling the pink blanket fully onto his lap to hide his own reaction to their activities.

Fred slid into the seat beside him. 'So. How's being a couple with Nell going?'

'Fine.' Alex sneaked a look up at his friend, and found a knowing glint in Fred's eye. 'Boring,' he added, not caring how obvious the lie was.

'Right.' Fred didn't even pretend to look convinced. 'Well, that's what I'll tell Polly when she asks, then.'

Relief surged through him. At least Fred wasn't going to tell his fiancée his suspicions—which meant Nell might let him live another day or two.

'Great.' Alex reached for his headphones. 'Now, if you don't mind, I've got a trashy movie to watch.'

'Sure. Just…' Fred hesitated, and Alex looked up at him again. 'Just be careful, yeah? For all our sakes.'

Alex grunted agreement, and turned his attention to the film playing on the screen in front of him.

But when Nell returned half an hour later,

in time for the meal service, he couldn't even have said what movie he'd been watching.

'What do you mean it's not here? Can you check again? Please?'

Nell rubbed the back of her hand across her forehead as she leaned heavily against the marble counter of the hotel reception desk.

Fourteen hours on a plane, then a transfer by car and—horrifically—helicopter to their private island, and Nell was at the end of everything. She couldn't even muster much enthusiasm for the incredible location Polly and Fred had picked for their wedding.

Alex had stumbled away to check the bridal villa was ready for Fred and Polly, who'd been whisked away for a relaxing welcome drink by the wedding planner, and then she imagined he'd be passing out asleep in his room for the next eight hours. She knew he hadn't slept on the plane, because after she'd returned from her conversation with Polly he'd stayed up to distract her by watching stupid movies with her and keeping a running commentary going, whispered by her ear, so she didn't concentrate on the fact they were miles up in the air in a metal box that could crash at any moment.

Naturally, she hadn't slept either.

She'd planned to head straight to her room and crash out too, but before she did she'd just wanted to check one simple thing.

That Polly's wedding dress, sent ahead by a specialist courier company, had arrived.

'I'm sorry,' the slender young lady behind the reception desk told her, looking very apologetic. 'It doesn't appear to be here. Perhaps you could try contacting the courier company.'

'I will do that. Thank you.'

As she turned away the luxurious hotel lobby started to spin, and she reached out for something to hold onto—only to find that someone had hold of her.

'Okay, I think you need to sit down,' Alex said, guiding her to a nearby chair.

She sank into its plush cushions gratefully. 'I thought you'd gone to sleep.'

'Without you?' He gave her a soft smile. 'I've only got one more week with you, and I have no intention of wasting any of it.'

She couldn't help but return his smile at that, before she even remembered to check that no one was watching them.

Alex sat back in the chair opposite her. 'So. What's the problem?'

'Polly's wedding dress hasn't arrived.'

Alex winced. 'Okay. What do we need to do?'

'I need to call the courier company, see what's gone wrong.'

'They're based in the UK?' Alex asked. Nell nodded. 'Then they won't be open for another couple of hours. I'll send an email to our London office and get someone to follow up on it the moment they get in. And you can get some sleep. Okay?'

It sounded so simple when he said it like that.

'I don't think my brain is working right now.'

'That's because this day has lasted approximately seven thousand hours.' Alex stood up again, rather creakily she thought, and held out a hand to pull her up too. 'Come on. Email then bed. Okay?'

She nodded and took his hand—then stopped, as the hotel doors opened again and two familiar people walked in.

Alex glanced back over his shoulder to see what she was looking at. 'Paul and Jemima?'

Nell nodded.

'You knew they were going to be here,' he said. 'Come on. You don't have to talk to them.'

But she did. Because she was the maid of honour and Alex was the best man, and part of their duties was greeting the guests when the bride and groom weren't there to do it.

Pasting a smile on her face, she crossed the lobby towards her ex and his new girlfriend.

'Paul, Jemima, so lovely you could make it.' She held out a hand to Jemima. 'I'm Nell, the maid of honour, and this is Alex, the best man. Shall we get you both checked in? I think you're staying in one of the gorgeous rooms here at the hotel.' Polly and Fred had booked out the place—plus the twelve private villas on the beachfront—for their guests.

She ignored any attempt from Paul to start a conversation, and instead listened to Jemima chattering on about all the things she wanted to do while they were in the Seychelles—including hiking, surfing, snorkelling…

'And of course I'd *love* to dive with sharks,' she said.

Nell couldn't resist a glance at Paul, who she happened to know had a deathly fear of most sea creatures. He was, she was pleased to note, looking rather green.

'Sounds like you've got a wonderfully *adventurous* week planned,' she said as she handed them over to the staff on the front desk. 'I know how keen Paul is to live a more adventurous, risk-taking life, after all.'

That was what he'd told her when he dumped her.

Served him right if he got eaten by a shark.

'That was fun,' Alex said as they walked away. '*Now* can we go to bed?'

'Definitely.' The adrenaline of dealing with her ex had worn off fast.

They made it all the way to the walkway that led to the private villas along the beachfront before they spotted the next arrival.

There, stepping out of a car in a wide-brimmed sunhat that must have annoyed everyone on the plane, was Madeline Andrews.

Her mother.

Nell froze as she watched the staff dancing attendance on her, rewarded by smiles and compliments, as Madeline was led towards the main lobby. Give her ten minutes and Nell knew that everyone on the island would be halfway in love with her mother.

Everyone except her, anyway.

She *had* to love her because she was her mother. But that didn't mean she had to like her.

And if she tried to talk to her now, for the first time since—wow, when was it? Two Christmases ago, maybe?—it could only be a disaster. She needed sleep before she faced Hurricane Madeline.

'Bed?' Alex asked, following her gaze.

Nell nodded. 'Yes, please.'

'Your wish is my command,' he said, and put an arm around her shoulders as he led her off to their private villa.

At least she could just take a few hours to rest in his arms, before she had to deal with her ex, her mother and a missing wedding dress.

CHAPTER FIFTEEN

ALEX WASN'T ENTIRELY sure why dealing with the missing wedding dress had become his responsibility, but there was no way he was waking Nell up to deal with it and, since she didn't want to panic Polly unnecessarily, nobody else on the island—barring the receptionist—actually knew it was missing.

So when the London office emailed back later that afternoon with the latest from the courier—insisting that the wedding dress had definitely been delivered on schedule as Polly had paid a lot of money for—he left Nell dozing in their bed and headed back to reception to instigate another search of the hotel.

'I'm sorry, sir, but there really is no sign of it—and no record of it arriving at all,' the receptionist said.

Alex sighed. 'Right. Any suggestions? Ideas?'

She looked around to check they weren't being listened to, then leaned across the counter. 'As it happens, my aunt is a seamstress on the next island. She does very nice work…'

'Right. Thanks.' Alex wasn't sure Polly was going to go for that one, given the amount of time and money she'd spent choosing her dress in the first place. 'You'll call me if the courier actually shows up, right?'

'Immediately,' the receptionist promised. 'You know, the courier might just have decided to wait until after the storm to fly it over from the mainland.'

Oh, good. Something else to worry about. 'Storm?'

She nodded. 'Apparently there's a tropical storm brewing. It probably won't reach us here, but…' She trailed off and shrugged.

'A tropical storm. Isn't it the wrong season for those?' He was sure he'd read something about them happening in January in Nell's guidebook.

She shrugged again. 'Weather.'

'Indeed.' A tropical storm. Just what this wedding needed.

He pulled out his phone to check the weather forecast as he turned away from the counter and almost walked into Jemima and Paul, who were approaching.

'Alex! Everything okay?' Paul sounded a

little desperate. 'Did I hear something about a storm? Should we batten down the hatches?'

The weather app at least was reassuring. 'It's probably going to miss us,' Alex said.

'Oh, good.' Jemima beamed up at him. 'I'm just about to book some trips for us tomorrow! I'd hate for them to be cancelled. What first do you think, baby?' she asked, turning her attention back to Paul. 'Diving or jet-ski tour of the islands?'

'Up to you, uh, darling.' Paul, Alex suspected, would rather have his wisdom teeth pulled than do either.

Served him right for thinking he could do better than Nell.

'Right, well, I'd better get back.' Alex waved vaguely in the direction of their villa. 'Have fun you two.'

Jemima was already at the desk enquiring about trips, but Paul hung back a moment and when Alex started to leave he reached out and grabbed his arm.

'Everything okay?' Alex stared at Paul's hand on his shirtsleeve until he let it go and stepped back, looking awkward.

'I just wanted to ask… You and Nell,' Paul said, stammering slightly to get the words out. 'I saw you together at the engagement party, and I wondered…'

Alex raised his eyebrows. 'Are you asking if we're together?'

'You just don't seem like her usual type, that's all,' Paul said stiffly. 'I was surprised.'

'Jemima hardly seems like yours either,' Alex pointed out. 'Everyone likes a change of pace sometimes, don't they?'

Paul shook his head. 'Not Nell. She likes things to stay exactly the same as they've always been, ever since she was old enough to take control of her own life. *You* are not the same.'

A part of him desperately wanted to tell Paul the truth—or a version of it, at least. That he and Nell *were* together, and no, things weren't the same, they were better than ever, and even though it seemed impossible, they *fitted...*

But he couldn't.

Because Nell didn't want anyone to know. Because, actually, things weren't different. She had every intention of going back to her little cocoon of boringness and security the moment this wedding was over.

She was basically using him for great sex, and while Alex had been fine with that when he was doing the same to her, now…

Something had changed. And he wasn't sure he wanted to examine too closely what that was, when there was nothing he could do to change the ending to this story.

So he stuck to the party line instead.

'No, we're not together,' he told Paul. 'Polly paired us up for the events as best man and maid of honour, that's all. We've got one of the two-bedroom villas on the beachfront as a reward.'

The relief on Paul's face was obvious, and it stung.

Is he going to try to win her back? Or does he just not want anyone else to have her, in case he needs a fallback plan?

Either way, it made Alex hate Paul just a little bit more.

'Alex?' Jemima called from the reception desk. 'Do you and Nell want to join us for a jet-ski tour tomorrow?'

Paul laughed. 'Nell would never do that sort of thing.'

'Maybe not. But Alex would,' Jemima said, eyeing him speculatively. 'I've heard stories about him.'

'Who hasn't,' Paul muttered, with an ominous glance in Alex's direction.

He ignored it.

Usually, he'd jump at the chance to try or do or see something new. To hang out with new people, who were open to new experiences.

If it was dangerous, or at the very least exhilarating, that only made it more appealing.

But this week he had other priorities.

'Sorry, best man duties,' he said. That sounded better than *I don't want to leave the woman who won't admit she's sleeping with me*, right?

He made his goodbyes and was heading back to the villa when he recognised another guest in the bar—Nell's mother.

As best man, he should probably introduce himself. Even if Nell had made it clear she wanted to keep her distance for now. He didn't know the whole story of the twins' relationship with Madeline, but while Polly obviously wanted her here for her big day, it was just as obvious that Nell would have been happier if she wasn't invited.

It was the sort of thing he'd ask Nell about, if their relationship was anything more than a short-term fling. As it was…he wasn't about to risk anything that might make her decide to end things earlier than planned.

Didn't I used to be the risk-taker in this not-a-relationship?

Before he could decide whether to introduce himself to Madeline, she was joined by another man—somewhere between Nell's age and her mother's, he guessed. When the man bent in to kiss Madeline, he decided that introductions could wait.

Madeline was clearly having a lovely time. Now he had to make sure that her daughter was too.

Guests continued to arrive all that day and into the next. Nell managed to coordinate things mostly from her villa, via the phone—including tracking down the courier, who had *clearly not* delivered Polly's dress as he claimed.

'It'll be there before the wedding,' he promised. 'Just relax and enjoy the island!'

As if relaxation was really an option, when her sister was getting married in just a few days, her mother was loose somewhere on the island doing heaven only knew what, and Nell herself was embroiled in a best man with benefits arrangement that—

Well, that was kind of wonderful, actually. Which was at least part of the problem.

Because it had to end. Really soon.

Before she got any more attached than she already was.

Nell knew that this wedding was littered with Alex's ex-girlfriends—somehow, he always managed to stay on good terms with them, and plenty of them had been part of their friendship group at university, so it was inevitable they'd see each other again. But the last thing Nell wanted any of them knowing was that she—sensible, stable, determined-to-be-boring Nell—had fallen for the same charms that the rest of them had.

Or that she was going to be cast aside the same as all the rest, for that matter.

It wasn't that she was embarrassed by her connection with Alex—she knew for a fact that it would improve her standing in the opinion of nearly everyone attending the wedding, in truth.

Especially her mother.

And *that* was what she wanted even less than a missing wedding dress or the humiliation of being another one of Alex's exes.

She just couldn't bear her mother telling her that she was a chip off the old block after all—falling for the handsome, daring, unpredictable best man. This fling was *exactly* the sort of thing Madeline would do—and Nell had spent most of her life fighting to be defined as the anti-Madeline.

Of course, Mum had actually run off with the best man at *her own* wedding once, which was far worse. And only meant that she'd lecture Nell about how she couldn't even rebel with the same style and panache as she did.

No. Madeline Andrews could never find out about Nell and Alex—and neither could anyone else.

They didn't need to. It would be over soon enough.

Shaking away her less than cheery thoughts, she headed out across the strip of sandy beach towards the main reception, to see what else could possibly go wrong with this week that she'd be required to fix.

This was why the world needed boring people, she decided. So they could put things right while the more adventurous and dramatic people were off having adventures and not caring about the basic but important stuff.

Like whether the bride had a wedding dress or not.

In fairness, it had been her decision to keep the news of its loss from Polly. But it did mean that her twin was now having a lovely time at the spa on the next island, while Nell had spent all morning on the phone to various couriers around the islands, and Alex…

Where was Alex, anyway?

As she approached the reception building she spotted him, leaning against the wooden post of the jetty, staring out at the ocean. His broad back faced her, and she could tell his arms were folded across his chest.

He looked…contemplative, which was not a state she was used to thinking of in combination with Alex McLeod. He was all action and movement and doing before thinking… at least in his personal life. She'd always assumed that he used up all his patience, methodicalness and calm in his work, so had none left for his private life.

But there he stood. Contemplating.

And Nell knew she had to find out what he was thinking about.

'You look very thoughtful,' she said, coming to stand beside him. 'Contemplating our tiny existence in an unbelievably large universe, or watching those girls in bikinis on paddleboards?'

'Neither.' Alex wrapped an arm around her waist and pressed a kiss to the top of her head. For a moment, she wanted nothing more than to lean into his touch, but then she remembered that everyone on this island was there for Polly's wedding, and the last thing she needed was a report getting back to her sister—or mother—about her getting cosy with the best man.

So she stepped away. 'Then what?'

'They said at reception that there was a storm coming in. It probably won't reach us here, but some of the guests were going out on a tour around some of the outer islands and, well, they're not back yet.'

Nell sighed. 'Guess we'd better go inside and start making some more phone calls then, huh?'

'Looks like.' He gave her a lopsided smile and offered her his arm as they walked inside.

And, despite all her reservations, she took it. Because he wasn't out there adventuring with the others—he was here, helping her fix things.

And maybe, just maybe, that meant something.

It turned out that the guests who'd gone on the adventure tour of the outer island had got themselves a little bit stranded. The receptionist looked grateful when Nell and Alex showed up to help with the phoning around to find someone willing to brave the storm to get them back. The storm was threatening to linger for a few days, and if they didn't get back in time for the wedding Polly would be livid.

'Did you not want to go with them?' Nell asked in a lull between phone calls, while they waited to hear back from someone who might be willing to make the trip. 'A jet-ski adventure tour of strange islands in a tropical storm sounds exactly the sort of thing you'd be jumping to sign up for.'

'They did invite me,' Alex admitted, wondering why she'd asked. Had she *wanted* him to go? Or was she hoping he'd changed his ways?

Or was she worried he'd stayed for her, when she didn't want him to?

'You turned them down?'

He shrugged. 'I had things to do here.'

'Very responsible,' she said, eyeing him with something unreadable in her gaze.

But then the phone rang again and the moment was over.

Eventually, they managed to get their wayward guests back to the island—looking a little tired and windswept, but otherwise none the worse for wear. Alex and Nell were there to meet them—and the courier finally delivering Polly's wedding dress—in the reception space.

'Well, at least we've got a great story to tell about our trip,' Jemima declared, laughing, as she strolled through—her hair windswept but her make-up still somehow flawless.

Paul followed behind her, looking significantly more dishevelled and, if Alex wasn't mistaken, rather disillusioned with the spirit of adventure he'd been courting when he left Nell for Jemima.

From the slightly smug smile on Nell's face when he turned to look at her, she saw it too. And in that moment he could feel any chance at a future with her slipping from his grasp.

What future? I don't want a future with Nell Andrews. Just a fling. That's what we agreed.

But Alex had never been very good at lying to himself.

With all the guests back where they belonged, and Polly's dress safely hung in the bridal suite, Nell slipped her arm through his and stretched up on tiptoes to whisper in his ear. 'I reckon we've got another couple of hours before the rehearsal dinner. Think they can manage without us out here for now?'

'Definitely,' Alex replied.

The future might be out of his grasp, but the present was very much in it. And hadn't he always preferred to live in the moment anyway?

Right now, at this moment, Nell was still his.

And he intended to enjoy every moment of that while it lasted.

CHAPTER SIXTEEN

FOR THE REHEARSAL DINNER, Polly and Fred had arranged a spectacular beachside event—one that had, thankfully, been facilitated by the tropical storm passing by the outer islands and moving back out to sea, without ever coming close to their venue. Nell wasn't sure her sister even knew of the storm's existence—she'd spent the day at the spa with her other bridesmaids, accepting Nell begging off only because she knew how much she hated sitting around and gossiping with most of Polly's other friends.

And since Nell had spent half the day rescuing guests from the storm, and the other half in bed with Alex, she'd decided that made the scales just about even.

Okay, maybe tipped slightly in her favour. Or a lot.

The chemistry between her and Alex still continued to amaze her—and the most surprising thing of all was that it didn't seem to be sizzling out over time.

If anything, it was only getting hotter.

So by the time she met Polly down at the beach before the dinner, to do a final check of the set-up, they were both relaxed and happy in their own ways.

'It looks beautiful.' Nell placed her hands on her hips and looked out over the carefully placed tables with the ribbon-wrapped chairs and the tropical flower and fruit centrepieces. Tomorrow, after the beach wedding itself, they'd be in the large courtyard in the centre of the hotel complex, with a fully catered five-course dinner being served from the kitchens nearby. There'd be musicians and a bar and a hundred other details Nell couldn't remember.

But tonight, the rehearsal dinner, was supposed to be lower key. Not all the guests on the island were invited, just the wedding party and close family—the rest had a buffet going on in the main restaurant. They had a guitarist and singer on a small dais near the tables, and a cocktail bar set up on the sand. The water lapped against the shore, calm and tranquil now all signs of the storm had passed.

Everything was perfect.

Polly clapped her hands together with excitement, her smile contagious. 'I can't believe we're really here, Nell. All the planning and waiting—'

'It's only been three months since Fred proposed, Pol,' Nell couldn't help but point out. Her sister ignored her.

'And now we're finally here! Tomorrow I'm getting married, and Fred and I will be together for ever, no matter what.'

Nell forced herself to keep her smile in place. 'You really will.'

She believed her words, that wasn't the problem. Maybe their mother had never managed to make a marriage last, and their father had had no interest in getting married in the first place, but Polly and Fred would make it. She was sure.

She just couldn't help but wonder if, just as Polly had got all the charm and adventurousness from their parents, she'd got the love and happiness quota that they should have shared too.

Nell had never truly been jealous of her twin before. But imagining her spending her life with the man who loved her beyond everything, and who she loved back just as fiercely—despite any disagreements or drama—that, well. That was worth envying.

She looked up and saw guests starting to

arrive, and shooed Polly off to get changed into her dress for the evening. Nell was already dressed in her own, black dress, sparkly silver sandals her only concession to the occasion, and the beachfront setting.

She smiled and welcomed Fred's family, relieved when Alex joined her as he knew them better than she did, so was more relaxed around them all. From Polly's side of the family, there weren't many people to know; most of her invite list had been friends rather than family, and tonight was meant to be family and wedding party only. Other than herself and the five bridesmaids, there was only an elderly great-aunt—the sister of their father's mother—and her daughter, and Madeline.

Who was, of course, late.

'She's probably waiting to upstage the bride and groom,' Nell told Alex when he asked where her mother was.

'She'd do that?' Alex sounded surprised. Which, given his own parents' behaviour at the engagement party, seemed rather naive.

'She lives for that,' Nell confirmed.

Just then, she saw two figures stumbling towards them. One was using the rope of fairy lights the hotel had used to mark the path as a rather insufficient hand rail.

'Here we go,' Nell said.

The figure gripping the fairy lights was male, and not anyone she recognised from the wedding party. The woman, however, in her lipstick-pink dress and high heels that sank into the sand, was instantly recognisable as her mother.

'Who's the guy?' Alex asked. 'Wait, I saw him kissing her in the bar before. Did we know she was bringing a date?'

Nell frowned. 'She didn't. She arrived alone.' And there definitely hadn't been a plus one on her invitation; even Polly wasn't as trusting as that. She'd paired Madeline up with Fred's widower uncle for all the wedding week events, since neither had made the engagement party or the hen and stag dos.

Leaving her post, Nell stepped forward to intercept them. 'Mum.'

'Nell! I haven't seen you yet!' She threw her arms around Nell's shoulders, and Nell smelled the alcohol on her breath. 'Nigel, this is my other daughter—the one who isn't getting married.' She dropped her voice and put a hand to the side of her mouth. '*Probably ever*.' They both laughed.

Nell's jaw tightened, but she ignored them, aware of Alex standing at her side. She didn't want to make a scene, although she knew her mother would love it if she did. That way, she'd be the centre of attention—which was just the way Madeline liked it.

'Mum, the rehearsal dinner is for family only,' she said firmly. 'If you want to say goodbye to your new friend now, Alex will show you to your seat.'

'You're with Fred's uncle Roger, Madeline,' Alex said, offering her his arm. 'He's looking forward to getting to know you.'

Nell hoped Uncle Roger was deaf. Otherwise he was going to know the whole life story of Madeline Andrews—probably heavily embellished to include extra name-dropping—before they'd reached dessert.

She'd expected Madeline to latch onto Alex as a younger, more handsome and eligible man—that was her usual modus operandi. But instead she took tighter hold of her companion's arm.

'But darling, Nigel *is* family! Or he will be, soon enough.' Madeline looked up into Nigel's eyes, every inch the besotted new lover. 'We're getting married, you see. Right here on this island! I just can't wait to tell everyone tonight. Or do you think we should save the news for the toasts at the wedding tomorrow?'

Nell felt her heart sinking down into the sand, and wished she could follow it.

This was what she'd been afraid of. Why she'd hoped Madeline wouldn't have been able to make it to the wedding for some reason.

Because of course her mother would want to make Polly's wedding all about her.

Never once, in all their childhoods, had anything been about them. Everything had to be about Madeline.

And now she was trying to steal Polly's most precious day from her.

Well. Not on Nell's watch.

And from the steely look in Alex's eye, not on his either.

'We absolutely cannot let Mum ruin tonight,' Nell hissed to Alex, as Polly and Fred approached the rehearsal dinner and the guests all stood and clapped. 'Or, more importantly, the wedding tomorrow.'

'Of course we won't,' Alex replied. 'But how, exactly, do you intend to stop her?'

From the little he'd seen of Madeline Andrews, she didn't seem to be the sort of person who took a hint. Or a direct command. Or any interest in what anyone else cared about or felt at all, actually.

How had such a woman created someone

as sensitive and caring as Nell? It really made no sense.

'Okay,' Nell said after a moment's thought. 'This is what we do.'

They averted the immediate crisis by a strategy of divide and conquer. Alex led Madeline over to sit by Uncle Roger, and had an extra seat added to the table so he sat on her other side, where he could keep an eye on her. The staff from the hotel restaurant didn't look too happy at the unexpected addition, but he promised to eat whatever they had left over.

Nell, meanwhile, dragged Nigel into Alex's original seat beside her, so she could keep tabs on him. Polly gave them both a slightly odd look as she took her own seat, but she didn't immediately question it. Alex shot Nell a relieved look across the tables between them, and she returned it.

By the end of the meal Alex knew far more about Madeline Andrews' varied and self-centred existence than he'd ever wanted to—and thought he might understand a little more about Nell because of it.

He'd assumed her need for security and boredom came from being abandoned by her adventurer father, but it seemed her mother was probably just as responsible. If she'd been present at the assassination of JFK, Alex was pretty sure Madeline would have told the story purely in the context of how she got blood on her favourite dress.

And while he was certain she *hadn't* been present that fateful day in Dallas—if only because she'd definitely have told the story if she had—she did seem to have a way of being in the right place at the right time. Well, if what she was looking for was drama, notoriety and stories to tell about famous people, anyway.

If the right place and time meant being with her daughters growing up, not so much.

Nell didn't want her own kids to grow up like she had. She wanted to give them a stable home with a boring, dependable dad. He could understand that.

And he could also understand why she wouldn't see him in that role. Hell, he wasn't even sure he wanted kids, if it meant putting them through what he had to put up with from his own parents.

So, all in all, the rehearsal dinner had just been another depressing demonstration of why he and Nell had to break things off once the wedding was over.

Less than forty-eight hours and we'll be on the plane home.

He glanced over at Nell again and wished he was sitting with her, as the table plan said he should be.

He didn't like wasting the last of their time together.

They made it through the meal without any last-minute declarations from Madeline or Nigel—something Alex put down to Nell's mother deciding the actual wedding would be a more dramatic occasion to announce things, anyway.

Alex made his way across to Nell the moment Polly and Fred had symbolically separated for the night. From here, they wouldn't see each other until they met at the altar.

'Do you need to stay with your sister tonight?' The bridal suite—where Polly and her bridesmaids had been set up for the night before the wedding—was on the second floor of the main hotel, and had the advantage of two bathrooms plus a dressing room, with plenty of space for the hairdressers and make-up artists to do their work.

Nell shook her head, and Alex's spirits rose just a little. 'She knows I don't always play nicely with others, so she said she was fine if I wanted my own space tonight—as long as I put on the stupid maid of honour dress tomorrow.'

'Not black?' Alex guessed.

'Not even slightly.' She sighed. 'But she's my sister. So I'll wear it anyway.'

That was Nell all over, Alex thought. She knew when things mattered, and when they didn't, and she gave her attention to the ones that did. It was one of the things he loved most about her.

Wait.

Not loved. Obviously.

Liked.

In a friendly way.

'You're a good sister,' he said, swallowing the sudden panic rising inside him.

Nell gave him a curious look. 'It's just a dress. And it's Polly's wedding, not mine. This whole thing…it's not about me.'

And that was the difference between Nell and her mother, he realised. He wanted to tell her as much. To tell her why she didn't have to worry about ever being like her—she couldn't if she tried.

He wanted to tell her so many things. But how could he, when this all ended the day after tomorrow?

Nell glanced around, then frowned. 'Where's my mother? And Nigel, for that matter.'

'They were right here…' Alex looked around too, but there was no sign.

'We need to find them.' Nell's eyes were wide with panic. 'What if they've gone to tell Polly they want a double wedding?'

'They wouldn't,' Alex said, before realising, yes, they probably would. 'Or they're planning to elope tonight and announce it tomorrow,' he suggested, and Nell groaned.

'Okay, I'll go check the bridal suite and the hotel bar; you go check the villas and the beach bar.'

'What do I do if I find them?' he asked.

'Just...make sure they're not causing a scene. And get them back to Mum's room as quickly as you can. Okay? Then I'll meet you back at our villa later.'

'I'll see you there.' With a quick check to be sure no one was watching, Alex ducked his head to kiss her, just once, on the lips. Then he turned to go and fix this latest wedding problem.

Because Nell had asked him to. And he was coming to realise there wasn't much he wouldn't do for her.

Which meant there might be another, more important, conversation they needed to have in the future, perhaps.

Nell trudged back to the beachfront villa she shared with Alex, her sandals in her hands.

She'd searched the whole hotel, and both bars, but there was no sign of her mother and Nigel. At least she'd also had the opportunity to check that Polly was having fun with her friends, and share a glass of champagne with them before bed.

Maybe it would have been nice to spend the night before Polly's wedding with her sister but, on balance, Nell knew she'd rather spend it with Alex—especially if it was the last night they got together. She'd never really gelled with Polly's friends anyway.

Now she just had to hope that Alex had found Madeline and Nigel, and averted any last-minute nuptials, or anything else that might cause drama on Polly's wedding day.

She paused outside the villa and looked out towards the ocean. Whoops of laughter floated towards her on the air, and when she squinted she could see people out there in the waves.

She moved closer.

Not just people. She recognised that bright pink dress. The one that a woman had just pulled off and thrown into the sea.

'Madeline!' She recognised that voice too. Laughing, not scandalised.

Alex.

Well, she'd told him to take care of her mother, she supposed. She couldn't blame him for doing whatever it took. She'd known her mother would like him. And that Alex would like her.

They were two of a kind. The adventurous, fun-loving kind.

The opposite of her.

Of course they'd connected.

Ignoring the burning sensation at the back of her throat, Nell turned and headed inside the villa. But she found she wasn't ready for sleep just yet, despite the late hour. Too many thoughts, perhaps.

Fixing herself a cup of herbal tea, she took it out to the small covered porch at the back of the villa, away from the sea. The porch was equipped with two light chairs and a small table between them. Placing her mug on the table, she took a seat and prepared to enjoy the peace and quiet before the chaos of the day ahead tomorrow.

The porch area looked out over a wide garden that her villa shared with all the other beachfront accommodation. Tropical flowers bloomed bright and proudly, standing out and drawing attention in a way that English wildflowers never did.

Nell could see why Polly had chosen this incredible place for her wedding; it suited her and Fred down to the ground. But she'd felt out of place since the minute she arrived.

She missed London.

She missed how simple things had been there, even after she and Alex started their fling.

It was strange to think she'd be going back to a whole new world—one where Polly was married and she and Alex were barely even friends, just business partners.

Could they really do that?

She wasn't sure any more.

Although since he'd gone night swimming with her mother and who knew who else, maybe he was already getting ready to move on, back to his old life, without her.

Maybe she needed to do the same. Focus on the life she really wanted to be living, and find a way to make it happen.

She took a sip of her tea and stared out at the garden again. In the middle there was a path which led eventually back to the hotel, and it was lit up by torches all the way. She tried to think of them as way markers, points along her life's journey, places she wanted to stop.

One of them burned brighter than the rest somehow, and she knew that one had to be Alex.

But what came next? Maybe dimmer, less exciting lights, but ones that took her where she wanted to go.

To a future with safety, security, predictability, just as she'd always wanted. The opposite of the life her parents had led.

A future she could trust to always be there. That was what she really wanted, wasn't it?

But as she stared at the path, she realised suddenly there was someone walking along it, towards her.

Someone she knew.

'I was hoping I'd find you still awake,' he said as he drew closer.

Nell got to her feet, frowning slightly. 'Is something wrong?'

Paul shook his head, a knowing smile on his lips. 'Quite the opposite, in fact. I feel like I'm thinking clearly for the first time in months. May I join you?'

Nell gestured to the empty chair beside hers, but he shook his head.

'I won't need that,' he said.

'Okay.' Nell frowned. Obviously he wasn't planning on staying long, which was fine by her. But *he'd* come to *her*. Why?

Nothing about tonight seemed to make any sense at all.

Then Paul dropped to one knee in front of her on the porch, and she felt her heart stop.

CHAPTER SEVENTEEN

It was late—very late—by the time Alex had finally managed to get Madeline out of the ocean, into a towelling robe he'd borrowed from one of the beach huts, and back to her room. They'd lost Nigel hours ago, possibly in the beachfront bar where he'd found the pair of them after the rehearsal dinner.

'It's too early to call it a night!' Madeline had declared. 'Come on. I want to go skinny-dipping!'

Alex had wanted to just leave them to it, and hope that the lifeguards were working as late as the bar staff. But he'd promised Nell he'd make sure she didn't cause any more trouble tonight, and that meant sticking with her until he'd got her back to her room.

Which, finally, he had. He'd even stuck around just long enough to hear her snores start to reverberate around the landing outside, before heading back to the villa he shared with Nell.

Coming from the hotel, it made sense to cut through the gardens to the back entrance. Madeline's room was at one end of the hotel, though, so the nearest exit led him along the outside of the garden rather than down the well-lit middle path. Which meant he was almost to the villa before he saw them.

Nell, hands clasped to her mouth as she stood over a man on one knee, holding out a ring.

Paul.

He'd known the idiot had seen sense, the moment he'd trailed in after Jemima following the storm debacle. He'd tried the adventurous lifestyle and decided it wasn't for him. Of course he'd gone back to dependable, wonderful Nell.

The only question was whether she'd take him back.

If he'd been asked the question a month ago, he'd have said no way. Nell had a healthy sense of self-respect, and she was hardly likely to come running just because her ex had decided that spreading his more adventurous wild oats wasn't for him after all.

What had changed? What caused that niggle of doubt, the fear in his chest, that she might say yes?

He wanted to believe it was because he

knew her better now, and knew from personal experience how much holding out for the right, stable and boring future mattered to her. A hell of a lot more than he did.

Despite all the chemistry between them, and the fun they had together, he knew that she wouldn't even consider giving a relationship between them a chance—because she still had her heart firmly planted in that future she'd been planning her whole life.

A safe, secure one that no parent or anyone else could whisk out from under her.

He'd like to think that Paul having done exactly that already, just a few months ago, would be enough for her not to fall for his act now. But if she wanted it badly enough...he knew she might.

And what right did he have to stand in the way of that future? She'd never promised him anything beyond tomorrow, anyway.

The surprise in her eyes that he could just make out, even from a distance, not to mention the hands to her mouth suggested she might be considering Paul's proposal, at the least. If Polly had seen it, he knew she'd have been planning the wedding already.

And maybe that was the right thing to do.

What probably *wasn't* the right thing to do was for Alex to slip into the shadows beside the next villa and watch what was clearly a private moment.

He did it anyway.

'I realised this week that I don't want the drama and excitement I thought I needed,' Paul said, up on the porch. 'I want the quiet moments, the peace, the…reassuring sameness you always gave me, Nell.'

Nell, Alex noticed, didn't say anything.

'I made a mistake,' Paul went on. 'Ever leaving you. It's not one I intend to make again. And that's why I'm asking you, Nell Andrews, if you'll be my wife. I can't promise you drama or adventure, but I can give you security and stability. Everything you always said you wanted.'

Everything she'd always said she wanted.

Everything she'd told *Alex* she wanted too.

Everything he couldn't give her.

Suddenly, Alex didn't want to watch any more.

He slipped silently away, back towards the hotel bar.

He couldn't compete with everything Paul was offering, and he didn't intend to try.

If Nell really did want that life, he was the man to give it to her.

If she didn't…

Well.

Alex wasn't giving up hope just yet.

But he would give her the space to decide the future she wanted, without trying to influence it.

However hard the wait was.

Nell stared down at Paul, at the ring box in his hand. Where had he even got that? Had he brought it with him, preparing to propose to Jemima?

She wouldn't put it past him.

'I know you won't want to say anything to anyone until after the wedding is over,' Paul went on, even though she hadn't answered him. 'You won't want to upstage Polly of course—not that anybody could, right?' He gave a laugh, and she remembered suddenly how often he did that—putting down Polly as if she must think the same about her sister really but not say it in public.

She'd always hated that. She and Polly might be different, but that didn't mean she had to disapprove of Polly's life.

But Paul hadn't ever understood that. Hadn't understood how they could be so close when they were so different.

Alex did. She pushed the thought away.

Alex wasn't here, and this wasn't about him, right now. This was about her future.

The one she'd just been contemplating when the man she'd assumed, until three months ago, she would spend her life with showed up with a possibly repurposed diamond ring.

'I know what this is, Paul.' Nell dropped back into her chair, putting herself at eye level with him. 'I've done this myself, more times than I can remember.'

Paul frowned. 'What do you mean? You've proposed to people? Who?'

'No!' Nell laughed, but she wasn't amused. 'That's not what I… What I mean is this. Proposing to me. It's not actually about me at all.'

'Who else could it be about?' Paul demanded.

'What I mean is, you scared yourself—or maybe Jemima scared you,' she went on. 'You thought you wanted the interesting, adventurous life that she leads, but when you tried to live it with her, you hated it. For her, getting stranded in a tropical storm was a story she could tell later. It was a life event. For you, it was miserable. And so you lurched away from her and back towards something safe and familiar. Me.'

'Is that so wrong?' Paul asked. 'Being with Jemima only showed me how perfect what *we* had together was.'

'If it had been perfect, you wouldn't have

needed to go off with her in the first place,' Nell pointed out.

She'd *thought* they were perfect together too. Thought that Paul could give her everything she'd ever wanted.

But the last couple of weeks had shown her she wanted things she didn't even know she could want, until Alex came along and gave them to her.

'Look, I know I've made mistakes, but we're both grown-ups, right?' Paul looked eagerly up at her, anticipating her understanding. 'That's what makes you so different from everyone else in your family, or at that company of yours. We make sensible, rational, safe decisions. *You* make good decisions, always. And forgiving me, and moving on, is obviously the right decision for both of us.'

He made it sound so obvious, except Nell knew better now.

Safe, sensible, secure...they meant different things to different people.

For Polly and Fred, their safety was in each other. In knowing that the other would let them live their life—feel their emotions, seek their adventures, act out their dramas—but always still be there in the morning.

For her mother, it was knowing that everyone would always be talking about her—

even if she didn't like what they were saying. Nell didn't know what had started that drive in her—maybe it was her and Polly's father walking away because she didn't matter to him. But Madeline needed to matter. She needed to be seen, to be known, to be important—to more people than just her daughters.

Nell hated that about her. But she had to accept it was who she was.

And for Alex…she didn't know what meant safety to him. What meant *home*.

She wasn't sure if he did either.

For her…she'd always assumed it meant a place and a person where nothing ever changed. Where she could rely on consistency and boredom to keep her safe.

But now she wondered.

'I don't think it is the right decision,' she said slowly. 'Not for me.'

'Forgiving me isn't the right decision?' Paul sounded incredulous. 'Nell, you can't honestly intend to hold onto a childish grudge like your mother would.'

He was playing on her fear of turning into her mother, she realised. But she knew now she never would. She wasn't that person.

She was herself. And she *liked* the Nell she'd been since Paul left.

'*Marrying* you would be the wrong decision,' she corrected him. 'For me, anyway. I don't love you, you see. And I'm pretty sure you don't love me either.'

'What *is* love?' Paul asked. She assumed it was rhetorical. 'You and I both know that the grand passionate love affair isn't enough. Love isn't drama and storming out then making up again. It's being sure of the other person, trusting them to look after you, to help you. To know what's really important in life. Isn't it?'

Nell blinked, as a number of things all fell into place inside her at the same time.

'Yes,' she said slowly. 'You're right. It is.'

'So you'll marry me?'

She smiled down at him. 'Not in a million years.'

Because she knew what love was now. She knew what she wanted from her future.

And she intended to get it.

Alex wasn't entirely surprised to find Jemima in the bar, given that the man she'd brought to the wedding was currently proposing to another woman on his porch.

She turned towards him as he approached. 'You looking for a little company tonight too?'

'Mostly just looking for a nightcap.' He

hopped up onto the bar stool beside her, though, as he indicated to the man behind the bar that he'd like a beer. What he really wanted was hard spirits, but that wouldn't go so well with getting up and being best man in the morning. So, one beer before bed it was.

Maybe Nell really had been a bigger influence on him than he'd thought. He sounded positively sensible, even to his own ears. Practically responsible.

To his surprise, he didn't hate it.

Behind them, the bar was open to the beach and he could hear the waves lapping against the shore. This place was, objectively speaking, paradise.

So why did he wish he was back in London, with Nell, and that they'd never come here at all?

Jemima was eyeing him speculatively. 'You're better off without her, you know.'

'I don't know what you mean.' The barman brought his beer, and Alex nodded his thanks.

'Yes, you do.' Jemima nudged him with her elbow. 'I saw the two of you at the fairground engagement party thing, and I knew then. Not to mention this week. The way you look at her...you're besotted. But you know you're not the right kind of man for her.'

'Maybe I could be.' Denying that he wanted to be seemed beside the point now.

'You and I…we're not like them. Paul and Nell, I mean. They're normal—ordinary people who care about… I don't know. Mortgages and pets, or something. We don't care about that stuff. We know that life is about more than paying bills and going to work until you die. It's about seeing things and travelling places and having adventures that people stuck in the corporate cycle could only dream of!'

'You realise I do actually have an office job,' Alex said mildly.

'Do you, though?' Jemima gave him a knowing look. 'The way I understood it, you invested enough money into that company when Fred and Polly were setting up that you'd never need to work a day in your life, just live off the dividends they make you. Maybe you like to keep your hand in by contributing a little legal advice from time to time, but it's hardly a *job,* is it?'

She was right, Alex knew. He also realised he'd spent more time in the office since Fred and Polly announced their engagement than he ever had before. Because he wanted to see Nell. To share tales of disastrous dates. To enjoy their budding friendship.

To see it become more.

If she married Paul, he knew he'd be avoiding the office again for the foreseeable future.

'I know it can be tempting.' Jemima had shifted closer, her thigh pressed against his on the bar stool. 'I almost fell for it too. Paul said he wanted an adventure, and I thought I could show him our life and he'd give up everything else to be with me. But he wasn't built for it, the same way Nell isn't. They're made for each other, those two. All they care about is security and living their boring, respectable little lives, where everyone thinks they're perfect.'

'You're wrong.'

'Am I?'

Alex looked away, thinking hard.

Yes, Nell valued security. She'd had an unstable, unloving childhood, and she wanted to build her future in a way that made her feel safe and loved. That was understandable.

And yes, she cared what other people thought and said—if she didn't, she wouldn't have been so worried about their fling getting out. But was that because she wanted to be *respectable,* or because she wanted her privacy, in a way her mother never had?

Because, despite her protestations to the contrary, Nell wasn't *boring.* She just wasn't.

She was fun and entertaining and passionate and intelligent and funny. She knew herself, and what she wanted. She was confident in both those things too.

She was so much more than he'd ever seen, until she'd refused to go to this wedding with him.

And he was in love with her.

Alex stood up. 'Yes, you are.'

And he was going to find Nell and tell her that. Because as much as her decision about whether to marry Paul or not was only hers to make, she deserved to have all the information when she made it.

Except then Fred's cousin came racing into the bar, looking frantic. 'Thank God I found you! You're the best man. *You* need to talk to him if you want this wedding to go ahead tomorrow. Come on!'

CHAPTER EIGHTEEN

NELL WAS UP early the next morning, not least because she'd barely slept. Alex hadn't returned to the villa at all the night before, as far as she could tell—and he certainly hadn't joined her in their bed.

Their last night had passed, and they hadn't even spent it together.

She got up and showered, determined to ignore the ache in her chest at the realisation that her fling with the best man was already over. This was Polly's wedding day, and that was all that mattered.

She'd arranged to meet the bride and bridesmaids in the suite at the top of the hotel bright and early, to allow plenty of time for hair and make-up before the afternoon service on the beach. By the time she made it up there, hoping that the make-up artist could do something about the shadows under her eyes, the other women were all lounging around in short cotton robes and fluffy slide slippers, drinking Prosecco.

'Nell!' Polly jumped up and embraced her as she arrived. 'I'm so glad you're here! Now it really feels like my wedding day.'

Nell forced a smile. 'It's going to be magical.'

And it was. Polly seemed too distracted to notice Nell's slight melancholy, and the buzz of excitement in the room couldn't help but lift her spirits. In fact, everything was perfect. Even their mother arriving to share the bubbly and tell tall tales about the many times she'd *almost* got married couldn't blunt Polly's joy.

Nell was glad. One of them deserved that happiness, and it was probably always going to be Polly.

Happiness meant taking risks. And Nell had never—would never—find anything or anyone worth taking that kind of risk for.

At least she hadn't ever expected to.

And now it seemed it might already be too late. Unless she was willing to take a really, really big risk.

She wandered over to the window as her mother told the tale of her almost-elopement in Vegas to a gaggle of rapt bridesmaids. She supposed if you hadn't lived the stories the first time around they were entertaining enough.

Nell looked out over the gardens outside the bridal suite, towards where her own beach-front villa sat, and then frowned. Was that Alex, storming out of the villa? Where was he going? He looked like he was heading for the hotel—had something gone wrong?

Then she spotted the other figure, halfway up the garden path, glancing back over his shoulder as he hurried towards the window where she stood.

Nigel. Her mother's erstwhile latest fiancé.

Nell glanced back at Madeline.

'Of course, next time I head to the altar, I know it will be for real this time,' her mother said, her gaze slowly drifting towards the window where Nell stood. 'Sometimes, true love is worth waiting for. You know?'

True love. With a man she'd met less than three days ago on this island, and when she was only planning on announcing her engagement to him to upstage the bride—her own daughter. This—*this* was why Nell hated the idea of playing the world for drama, for the stories she could tell afterwards.

Because someone else always got hurt because of them.

Rage started to boil in her chest, and she

was about to turn on her mother when she realised that would only create a scene—exactly what Madeline wanted, and Polly wouldn't. Besides, Alex was still moving, barrelling towards Nigel at speed. Her eyes widened.

'Excuse me, just one moment,' she said, edging towards the door.

Just then, Polly appeared in the doorway, fully dressed in her wedding gown for the first time. 'Well, how do I look?'

'You look amazing, Pol,' Nell said honestly.

Then she used the excited buzz of the other bridesmaids gathering around to dash outside and find out what the hell was going on now.

'Nigel, we talked about this.' Alex stalked behind the older man as he hurried through the gardens. He could catch up and take him down easily, but he didn't want to if he didn't have to. Rugby tackling a second-hand car salesman to the ground was the sort of thing that drew attention, and that was something he was trying to avoid.

Which was why he'd spent the whole night with Nigel in his hotel room, making sure he didn't do anything stupid.

Ever since Fred's cousin had found him the night before, and told him there was a lunatic trying to get in to see Fred and arrange a joint wedding for him and the bride's mother, Alex had been on Nigel watch. They'd assumed that Madeline would be their biggest worry, but it turned out she'd managed to find a new man with an even bigger flair for the dramatic than hers.

Unless this was all her idea, of course, which was a possibility Alex wasn't ready to discount just yet.

So instead of spending his last night with Nell, he'd spent it listening to Nigel talk about his failed first marriage, the kids who didn't want to see him, the way his life just hadn't turned out like the dreams in his head, how he'd always been meant for bigger things—and how Madeline was about to make that happen for him.

It hadn't left him in the best mood.

Still, he'd dragged Nigel with him when he went back to the villa he and Nell shared to change for the wedding ceremony—only for the idiot to make a break for it while Alex was in the shower.

Now he had to get him back inside, where he couldn't cause any trouble, before Madeline, Polly or—worst of all—Nell saw him.

'I need to show them that I truly *love* their mother,' Nigel said, still hurrying along the path. 'I know it's only her daughters holding

Madeline back. But if I can show them—with a grand gesture—that my love is sincere, we can all be one happy family! I'll finally have the future I deserve.'

Alex had some thoughts on the future Nigel deserved, and he suspected they didn't match the pictures in Nigel's head.

Apparently reasoning was getting him nowhere, so Alex picked up the pace and grabbed Nigel by the arm—just as Nell appeared in the doorway from the hotel.

'What the hell is going on out here?' She folded her arms across her chest, and Alex took a moment to appreciate her in the pale blue bridesmaid's dress Polly had chosen.

She looked beautiful, of course. But he preferred her in black. It suited her better.

'Nigel wants to make a grand romantic gesture,' Alex said drily. 'I'm trying to convince him not to.'

'But I need to show you, your sister and your mother, how much I love her!' Nigel insisted.

'Today?' Nell asked. 'On her daughter's wedding day? You don't think that's a little unnecessary?'

Nigel shook his head. 'It's perfect! Madeline said—'

Nell and Alex rolled their eyes in unison.

'Of course she did,' Nell muttered.

'She said that she needed to *know* I love her, and then she'd marry me on the spot!' Nigel beamed. Alex wondered if he was still drunk. It would explain a lot.

Or maybe a woman like Madeline just messed with men's senses.

He didn't know why. She couldn't hold a candle to Nell.

'Do you realise how many other men she's promised to marry over the years?' Nell asked. 'She loves being engaged, but most of the time she never quite makes it to the altar.'

'That's why I need to marry her *today*,' Nigel said, as if he'd played a trump card. 'When it's true love, why wait?'

'Because this is crazy?' Nell said, but Nigel clearly wasn't listening.

Before Alex could make a grab for him, he'd darted forward and started to climb the trellis of tropical flowers that scaled the wall up to the window of the bridal suite. As Alex looked up, he saw Madeline and Polly both looking out of the window—one with glee, the other horror—at the man approaching them.

Alex moved forward to follow Nigel, but Nell's hand on his arm held him back. 'You'll be too heavy,' she said. 'The whole thing will fall. Besides, it's too late. Look.'

She was right, he realised, looking around the gardens. The wedding guests had already come out to see what the fuss was all about—and seemed to be loving the drama of it all. Only Polly, up in the window, and Fred, over by the honeymoon villa, looked unhappy. Polly seemed on the verge of tears, and Fred…well, Alex wasn't sure he'd ever seen his friend so angry.

The only thing Nell had asked was that he help her keep Polly and Fred's wedding day perfect. It was his job—as best man, as their friend and as…whatever it was he was to Nell.

And he'd failed.

Madeline was clutching some flowers from the trellis to her chest as Nigel loudly professed his love to everyone in earshot, and Polly's perfect wedding was ruined.

In that moment Alex hated drama and everything that went with it just as much as Nell did.

But then, just when he thought things couldn't get any worse, the trellis began to creak.

And crack.

And start to pull away from the wall…

Oh, God, the whole thing was going to come down—with Nigel still on it.

Nell called up to her mother to grab Nigel's

hands, but she was too busy shrieking dramatically. Polly reached for him, but a moment too late, as the trellis finally parted company with the wall holding it and it arced backwards, towards the ground, Nigel still hanging on. And screaming.

Somehow, Nell suspected this wasn't quite the romantic gesture he'd planned.

A few guests rushed forward to try and stop the descent, but it was quickly apparent it wasn't going to work. Which was when Nigel decided to jump.

The trellis had been falling so slowly it made Nigel's leap seem even faster, and more sudden. Nell's eyes widened as she watched him fall—and as she realised, too late, where he was going to land.

I need to move.

The thought filled her brain, but she couldn't convey it to her feet. Couldn't draw her eyes away from the falling man, or the inevitability of what was about to happen.

She was frozen, the way she'd always felt as a child, whenever her mother did or said something so awful that everyone stared, and all Nell could do was stand there and be laughed at.

And her mother's awful next fiancé was going to land on top of her.

Except suddenly she *was* moving—and not of her own accord.

Alex swept her into his arms and out of Nigel's path, leaving him to land hard and skid into the middle of a bush of tropical flowers.

Her heart racing, Nell stared up into Alex's eyes. It was exactly the kind of over the top, dramatic rescue she hated in movies—and now the assembled crowd was cheering and whooping for them, as Alex held her in what could only be described as a dip.

He could have just grabbed my arm and pulled me out of the way.

Except…she was glad he hadn't. She was *glad* he'd given her the romantic rescue—and not just because it took attention away from Nigel and her mum.

And before she could stop herself she was kissing Alex, in front of a cheering crowd, and she just didn't care who saw it.

CHAPTER NINETEEN

THE WEDDING WAS BEAUTIFUL, Alex expected. He honestly hadn't been able to pay enough attention to what was going on around him to really tell. He'd smiled, handed over the rings and everything else he was charged to do as best man, but beyond that…

Beyond that, all he could think about was Nell, and that kiss.

After they'd broken apart, she'd murmured something about talking later, then disappeared back up to Polly's room—and he hadn't had a chance to speak with her since. Even now, she stood at the other side of the happy couple, not looking at him.

Did she regret it? Kissing him where everyone could see? She hadn't *seemed* to, in the moment—which gave him hope. And he was pretty sure she wouldn't have kissed him at all if she'd said yes to Paul's proposal the night before. But beyond that? He had no idea what was going on.

Nigel had been carted off to the medical centre to be checked over, but Madeline had declined to accompany him—which Alex suspected might mean the double wedding was off, thankfully. Instead, Nell and Polly's mother sat in the front row of the congregation, dabbing her eyes with a handkerchief as Fred and Polly held hands on the sand and said their vows. He had a feeling the handkerchief might actually belong to the vicar, who was the recipient of many of Madeline's smiles.

He flipped mentally through all the stories she'd told him at the rehearsal dinner. He was *pretty* sure Nell's mother had never been engaged to a vicar before.

After the ceremony came the photos, and the wedding breakfast, and all the other perfect little details Polly had arranged that Alex didn't care about. He just wanted to talk to Nell, except every time he tried someone seemed to thwart him.

Before he knew it, it was time for the speeches. Thankful he'd prepared his weeks before, he pulled his notes from his pocket to look over them again—but stopped when he realised that Nell had taken the microphone.

'It's not always traditional for the maid of honour to make a speech,' she said. 'But Polly asked me to and…it's not often you get the chance to say lovely things about your closest friend in front of people who genuinely care and want to listen, so I thought I'd take the opportunity.'

Alex smiled, and realised that everyone else there was too.

'Our whole lives, no one has ever had trouble telling Polly and me apart,' Nell went on. 'Even though we're identical. We might look the same, but everything else about us is different. If there's an adventure to go on, a chance to take, Polly will take it—and I'll hide away at home. If there's a bright colour to wear, Polly will wear it, whereas I'm always in black—today being a notable exception,' she added, looking down at her bridesmaid's dress. 'It's always worked well for us, that gulf between our personalities. We've never been jealous of each other because we always wanted different things—and supported each other to get them. As much as I love Fred as a brother, I'd never want him as a husband!' The wedding guests laughed, even as Fred pretended to be offended, and Polly buried her head in her hands.

'But for the first time, this week I've been envious of Polly. Not because she's getting married in this beautiful place, and not even because all of you lovely people are here to celebrate with her.' Nell paused and looked around the assembled company, and suddenly Alex felt her gaze on him. 'I envied Polly her courage. Because it takes a lot of courage to fall in love. Love is a risk—it's giving your heart to another person, and trusting them to take care of it. To love it and cherish it and protect it as well as—better than, even—their own. And it's a challenge too, because suddenly you receive their heart in return, and you have to take care of that just as well.'

She held his gaze, and in hers Alex saw universes of possibility. His heart started to swell, and his hopes rise, in return.

He watched Nell's throat bob as she swallowed and looked away before continuing.

'I know that Fred and Polly together are up to that challenge. And I know that Polly has always been the brave one—that's why she found her happy ever after so early, and has gone after it so determinedly. And it's why they're the best couple I know—and I wish them every possible happiness in the future.' She raised her glass. 'To Polly and Fred!'

Alex raised his glass and echoed her words—and knew he had to talk to her.

'And now, the best man!' The master of ceremonies' voice rang out, and Alex got shakily to his feet to make his own, prepared speech—one filled with humour and affection, and nowhere near as much truth as Nell's.

But the moment it was over…he was going to find her.

And they were both going to be brave.

Alex caught up to her on the dance floor, just after Polly and Fred had their first dance. Nell had to admit, she'd been waiting for him.

'Nice speech,' she told him as he swept her up in his arms and out onto the dance floor.

'Yours was better,' he replied. 'Braver.'

'It's a new thing I'm trying.'

They danced for a few moments in silence, and Nell just enjoyed resting her head against his shoulder and feeling his body against hers.

Then Alex said, 'I saw Paul visit you last night.'

Nell pulled back and stared up at him. 'Is that why you didn't come back to the villa? Because you thought—'

'No.' He tugged her close again and swayed them gently. 'I *was* coming back, after I'd given you time to have whatever conversation you needed to have with him. But then Fred's cousin collared me and told me that Nigel was demanding to see Fred to ask for it to be a double wedding. So I spent the night babysitting him.'

Nell groaned. 'If I never see that man again…'

'I know how you feel,' Alex agreed. 'Although, given that your mother is now dancing with the vicar, we might all be spared Nigel as your new stepfather.'

'Thank goodness.'

'So, you turned Paul down?' Alex asked.

'Emphatically.'

'Can I ask why?'

Nell paused in their dancing again, and looked up to meet his gaze.

This was it. Her moment to be brave. If she couldn't do it now, then none of the rest of it mattered anyway.

'Because he wasn't you,' she said. 'Because…everything I thought I wanted—boredom and stability and everything—it wasn't *wrong,* exactly, it just wasn't the whole truth. I wanted those things because I was too scared to ask for more. Too scared to risk anything for love when I knew how ridiculously people behaved for it. Because I thought love had to be drama and arguments and pain and tears.'

'Like my parents,' Alex murmured. 'I thought for the longest time that arguments and drama just meant passion—that a relationship without those things wasn't worth having anyway. But I realised that what mattered most was what was underneath those things. That if you had trust and respect and love, then everything else was just…'

'Drama?' Nell suggested.

He laughed. 'Yes. And I *like* a little drama and adventure in my life. I won't deny that. But what I want more than that is the real stuff. The trust and respect and love.'

'And I *like* a little boredom and stability,' Nell replied. 'But I want the real stuff more too. And if it comes with a little drama… maybe I could live with that too.'

'Really?'

'I think…' She took a deep breath. 'I think I'd like to try. If you'd like to try with me.'

Alex's smile was soft. 'Honestly? I'm so in love with you, Nell, I don't think I could do anything else.'

He loved her. He really loved her. 'Enough to stay home on Friday nights with me?'

'If you'll go out someplace new and exciting with me on the Saturday,' he suggested.

'Deal.' She squeezed his hands, realising they were just standing in the middle of the dance floor staring at each other now. 'Because I love you too, in case I hadn't mentioned it.'

'You hadn't,' Alex said. 'But the kiss earlier was a clue.'

'It was meant to be.'

'Good. So…' He slipped his arms around her back again. 'Are you ready to try being brave together?'

'More than ready,' Nell said, her heart beating double time in her chest at the thought.

And this time, when he dipped her and kissed her, she was prepared for the way the whole room cheered.

This time, she was ready for anything.

Even love.

* * * * *

If you enjoyed this story, check out these other great reads from Sophie Pembroke